Broken by Love

Broken by Love

SHALAKA NADHE

Srishti
PUBLISHERS & DISTRIBUTORS

Srishti Publishers & Distributors
A unit of AJR Publishing LLP
212A, Peacock Lane
Shahpur Jat, New Delhi – 110 049
editorial@srishtipublishers.com

First published by
Srishti Publishers & Distributors in 2021

10 9 8 7 6 5 4 3 2 1

This is a work of fiction. The characters, places, organisations and events described in this book are either a work of the author's imagination or have been used fictitiously. Any resemblance to people, living or dead, places, events, communities or organizations is purely coincidental.

The author asserts the moral right to be identified as the author of this work.

Printed and bound in India

Dedicated to my mother
who never stopped being positive
and my husband
who never stopped loving.

Sushmita and her Monday mess

Mornings are always so chaotic. No matter how well you plan, things will go wrong if they have to. Murphy's Law, they say.

She had tried to wake up earlier than usual, but working late nights had not helped. She was drowsy and her body seemed to be aching all over. She felt her head was spinning and even two cups of strong filter coffee had done no good. She was still not feeling up to it.

If only she had woken up a few minutes earlier, she could have avoided the chaos that day. But now, she had no option but to run and make things work the way she had planned.

Sushmita was tired and drained. It was so hard for her to leave her cosy bed. It took her some time to be fully awake and get out of bed, but there are no exemptions in life. You've got to do what you've got to do. That was always what she told herself.

'Today is the last hectic day,' she thought. Once the presentation was over, she would be relatively free. It took her a while to convince herself to leave the warm blanket. Sumit and Amey were still in bed, as if the clock did not exist. Plus, they were already late.

It was Sushmita's ritual to cuddle up in bed with Sumit and Amey for a few minutes before their day started. They would have a tight family hug to remind each other that they would love and care for each other in every situation, no matter how grim the day. Today the family hug was replaced by some shouting and yelling in panic, to wake up Sumit and Amey.

Sushmita worked with a reputed multinational company. She was an engineer and had been building her career slowly and steadily. She was married to Sumit, her first love and had a lovely son named Amey. Sushmita was an attractive woman with a charming personality. She had curly long hair that she usually tied up in a bun. Her lotus eyes, highlighted with a thick line of kohl were the most lively part of her face. Her well-nourished, flawless skin was smooth and radiated like silk. An average height of 5'3" combined with her beautiful chubby face gave her a girl-next-door look. Sushmita carried a lot of mommy fat which gave her luxurious curves at the right places. She was cute and cuddly and she knew it. She knew that she needn't put in extra effort to look good. Though she had tried several things to lose weight umpteen times, she could never manage it. She had inherited the curves from her mother.

Sushmita was satisfied with her life. She was hardworking and intelligent, with a heart of gold and contagious positivity. She was a happily married, working woman and a proud mother who had it all, and she cherished it.

Being an ambitious, working mother, though, is not child's play. It requires you to have a heart of steel. No matter what, you just cannot stop. There are no excuses and no shortcuts at work. Her days started with creating a check-list of tasks and ended with ticking out those tasks.

Amey, her little one, had started his second term that day, and had to reach school on time. After a week-long break, he was lethargic. He wasn't very fond of school, which always created trouble in the morning.

It had been a mad house since morning. She was late, Amey was cranky, and there were numerous chores to be done.

Amey refused to get up and enter the bathroom. He still had to be bathed and dressed; his food still was to be cooked. The lunchboxes had to be packed. Amey was hauling for background music. "Mama, please let me stay at home with you today. I hate school. I will be a good boy, mama." He must have said "mama" a hundred times.

Sushmita was already exhausted. A tired mother running late, still could not be angry.

She finally promised Amey chocolates and ice-cream, and a visit to his favourite park along with a hundred non-achievable things and finally managed to get him out of bed.

Sumit needed tea first thing in the morning. He didn't enter the kitchen today, thanks to the chaos. He did not want to risk getting yelled at by Sushmita.

The clock was ticking a tad too fast. Sushmita was having palpitations, because of the anxiety of her presentation, coupled with the delay.

After a lot of shouting and running around, Sushmita had no choice but to run towards the school bus carrying Amey in one arm, his school bag and water bottle in the other. She handed over Amey to the lady in the bus after a lot of resistance from him and climbed down the bus. Just then, she realised that she was still carrying Amey's water bottle on her shoulder, and had forgotten to give it to him.

She climbed onto the bus again to hand over the bottle to Amey, almost out of breath.

The annoyed bus driver kept asking her to hurry up, impatient because other vehicles were honking at him.

'Why can people not just be more patient and understanding,' she thought. 'There are kids on the street with panicking parents running round.'

Sushmita was annoyed, yet she just waved her hand at the black sedan whose angry driver was honking at the school bus. What was the hurry? Why couldn't he just wait?

'I could not even kiss my baby goodbye,' she thought. Parting with your little child, even if it is for a couple of hours, is quite a challenge for mothers. She hated this part of the day most, when she had to send little Amey away to school. He made it even more difficult for her by the hauling and tears dropping from his eyes. Her heart would ache every single time she had to do that. How she wished she did not need to send him away from her even for a short time. But again, what needs to be done, needs to be done. She was late and upset, but people on the streets were not at fault here. The entire scene of dropping Amey inside the school bus, climbing up and down had taken a good ten minutes. She should have left the house sooner. She realised that now.

By now, there were many more cars lined up behind the black sedan. All honking, all cursing.

Success does not come easy

Sushmita was not only a charming young woman, but also a very hard working one. She was dynamic and focused, giving her best to every task. She was known for her hard work and passion to deliver nothing but the best.

It had been over a year-and-a-half that she had been working on a project of creating a software product, with a team of fifteen people. The project had been extremely complex, and the time in hand was not enough. Last year had been very hectic for the entire team. They had worked long hours to complete the project within the unrealistic deadline.

Sushmita and her team had finally completed the project and it was now time to present it to the client and get their final approval.

She had been waiting for this day, and preparing for it since weeks.

It was finally time to showcase all the hard work that she and her team had put in. The team had pulled frequent all-nighters, and she had spent countless sleepless nights designing and reviewing the product herself.

Numerous team meetings, peer reviews, testing and dry runs had finally delivered a successful software. She had been closely working with her team to collate all the data and had managed to make a presentation the previous day.

A grand meeting room was booked, the presentation was well prepared and she had read it over a hundred times in her mind. She had also invited her entire team for the presentation. It was her way of showing them how each and every one had played an important role in the success.

Her heart had been racing that whole week. The way it did years back, when she had to take a maths exam. The way it did the first time she drove her car.

The day had finally come and today she would get over with it. She had already planned that as soon as the meetings got over, she would rush home to Amey and make his favourite chocolate pancakes. She had been so busy in the last few days that she had hardly spent any quality time with him. She would make it up during the weekend, she thought. She would probably take him to McDonald's for some French fries and cheesecake. Or she could just play board games with him or they could watch a movie or something. All these ideas were racing in her mind. But first, she had to give a good presentation.

Hurry makes a man worry, but not always

Raghav had hit the gym by 5 a.m. as usual that day. After a good workout for an hour-and-a-half, he was famished. He realized he had forgotten to carry his protein shake. His cook had prepared it for him, but he had left it on the table.

Monday morning routine was always a little different for Raghav. After the workout, he would meet his father for breakfast. It was a weekly affair that he never missed. Every Monday, after working out at his favourite gym, he would drive to his father's house.

Unlike every Monday, that day he decided to take a different route to his father's house, and had no idea how crowded it would be because of all the housing societies around.

The traffic was congested, cars were screeching and people were honking. He waited for a while but the traffic did not seem to be clearing. He decided to get down to find out what was happening. Well, some school bus had blocked the road, and there was some chaos happening around the bus. He tried to overtake the bus but it was a narrow road and Raghav realised he was stuck. That is when he heard someone shouting about school kids and their parents.

Parents! These were a section of society that always confused him. He was annoyed beyond limits now, and wanted to annoy the bus driver too.

He was already running late, and some crazy woman was climbing up and down the bus, like it was a game. He was really frustrated. A million thoughts ran through his head. 'Why can't parents be a little more organized? Do they realize that people have more important things to do? Blocking the entire road early in the morning is not done. People have schedules, unlike these women who molly coddle their kids the whole time.'

He kept honking, hoping the bus would move, but it fell on deaf ears. The driver wouldn't budge. He had no option but to wait.

Just then, he saw a hand waving at him, requesting him to wait. A minute later, a beautiful woman got down from the bus, waving at him apologetically. She was a complete mess, still in her pyjamas, with hair tied in a messy bun, sunken, tired eyes, and no energy to move. 'This woman can fall anytime,' he thought.

Yet, there was something striking about her. It was nothing that he could point out, but she had a personality to die for. She reflected elegance beyond description and confidence beyond comprehension. One look at her and you could tell that she was humble, yet so confident.

She hurriedly ran towards a residential complex. She ran as if she was running a marathon and every second was important.

By now, Raghav had stopped honking, and did not realise that he was staring at her. After a few minutes of being in a trance, he finally came back to reality. By now, the roads were empty, but Raghav's heart was full of strange feelings and even stranger thoughts.

Raghav – the mystery

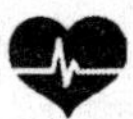

Raghav was a businessman who had worked his way up. His father owned a retail firm. Although he had been successful in making a good fortune with his business, he never expanded it. After his wife's death, Raghav's father could neither really concentrate on his business, nor did he have enough time for his son.

Raghav had always been a very bright student. He studied in good schools followed by a good university and had travelled to a few countries to understand international markets.

Initially he had worked as an employee in some companies to acquire basic knowledge about the corporate world and other commercial aspects. He had slowly learned the tricks of the trade. He would read and learn and had gained all the knowledge he needed to join his father's business.

Even after joining his father's business, he always wanted to make it big in life. He knew that the firm had a lot of potential to expand, but his dad had neglected it over the years. Slowly and steadily, Raghav started exploring different investment opportunities, and eventually, he had diversified the business and expanded it to make his father's small firm into a multinational company.

Over the last few years, he had grown his business in multiple domains to make his company a brand in itself. The Mehta Group had now ventured into construction, retail, import and export. Diversification of portfolio was the ethos of his business. Having multiple income streams was his idea of becoming rich. His dedication and passion had given fruitful results. He was vigilant and kept himself well-informed about the markets. He had an eagle's eye on capturing every opportunity to earn more income.

Raghav had also built a very strong network of people. He had developed a deep understanding of how to know a person's personality in a few minutes. He could literally read someone like a book, within seconds. His work made him travel often and meet people from varied backgrounds, so he had developed an inherent sense of analysing people. This art had helped him umpteen times in his business in the last few years.

It did not take him too long to capture all the details of the woman he saw today. She was anything but ordinary. She was a lady with immense strength and intense passion. He was impressed with her in the first sight. She was not in the best state, but Raghav instantly felt a strong attraction towards her.

Raghav knew how quickly he would get attracted to women. He brushed away his thoughts about the woman he saw and quickly altered his plans. He decided to cut his breakfast short and drive to work with his father. He had to sign some documents for the recently-acquired land amidst a beautiful valley.

He now wanted to venture into the hospitality business. A resort so beautifully done, that it would attract tourists from all around the world. He had been working really hard, planning each and every element of the hotel himself, to ensure that nothing went wrong.

The project was undertaken at a very large scale. His company had not reached a level where he could fund the project himself. He had invested a huge amount from his profit in the initial phase of the project, but now, he needed external investors. This was his dream project. If it succeeded, it would take him and his company to greater heights.

As per the plan, he would soon be flying across a few continents to pursue these investors and partners. He knew some of them personally, and some were introduced to him from his network.

Raghav had been really stressed over the last few months over the acquisition of this land. It was the most important, yet the most problematic milestone. Finally, this milestone of the project was also complete. With the property documents signed and the architecture plan sanctioned, the project was ready to launch. Launching the project officially meant he could now pursue investors.

With such stressful and ambitious thoughts already invading his mind, he had very little time to think about this unknown woman.

Everything had to go as per the plan. Time was money and Raghav would never lose money. He had set deadlines for each milestone and so far the project was on schedule.

He had invited a few people for the launch party and had formally announced the commencement of the hotel construction. His Personal Relationship manager and girlfriend Ayesha had made all the arrangements.

Everything has a story

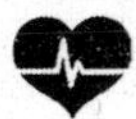

Ayesha was one of the most dynamic associates he had ever worked with. Blessed with a beautiful body and great intelligence, she had successfully managed his social image.

She was the kind of woman every man dreamt of. Her sensuous body and social skills had helped him develop a good network of businessmen. For Raghav, Ayesha was a good investment who could manage his work, and keep him happy too. He could take her along to social gatherings, with pride and ease. Her luscious body fascinated him, and would always fulfil Raghav's desires. She was a combination of beauty with brains.

She knew that Raghav would never commit to her and that she was merely an investment for him. Someone he could flaunt at parties and who would help him get introduced to various people. Deep down, they both knew he would never love her. Rather, he would never love anyone.

Love for Raghav was an unexplored territory. Having been brought up by nannies, Raghav's childhood memories had destroyed his faith in relationships. The absence of his mother during his growing years had made him so bitter that he had never actually experienced love. For him love and lust were synonyms and since lust came so easy, love always remained unknown to him.

He had heard that his mother was a fine woman. His parents had been from different backgrounds, different by religion and culture. Raghav's mother was half British. His maternal grandfather had stayed back in India even after the British had left the country. He had married his Indian grandmother. Raghav, hence, had unique features, a rare combination of European and Indian ethnicity. He was tall and fair like his mother, and had sharp features and beautiful eyes like his father.

Raghav's father could never make peace with the death of his mother, either. He had met her in college, and they both had fallen in love instantly. They were madly in love with each other until his mother succumbed to cancer, and little Raghav was left a motherless child.

His mother was a very strong woman; she battled her disease bravely. However, she could not take it too far. Her last days were extremely traumatic for the family. The hospital visits and her failing health had left his father emotionally disturbed. He had tried hard to play a dual role – of a strong father and a loving mother – but did not succeed.

His father tried his best to ensure that Raghav got the best upbringing, but he could never replace his mother.

As a child, Raghav longed for his mother's love. He longed to be a part of a complete family. Children his age would be fed and cared for by their mothers. Their dads would be around to teach them cricket and play football or ride a bicycle. Most of his friends used to be busy with their families during vacations and festivals. Those times were the toughest for him. No one would want to spend time with him. He would be left all alone. His father didn't care much about festivals, and barely noticed that he had vacations. He was always left under the care of nannies.

For a caretaker, a child is just a task. Rarely would someone identify his need of love. As a child, he felt lonely and deprived of love. He would outgrow the toys and the books very fast. The fancy things that belonged to him were no longer interesting. With nothing else to do, he would spend hours reading. With no one around, he would often speak to himself and pretend that there were other kids around him.

Slowly, his mind started playing games. He started imagining things. The pretend games were no longer restricted to game time, instead they became a part of his routine. Imaginary family and friends started following him everywhere and when he would realise that his imaginary world was different from reality, he would lose his temper, and throw tantrums.

Eventually, he became so temperamental that the nannies started avoiding him. They kept their interactions minimal, leading to more loneliness. It became a vicious cycle – temperamental issues because he had no friends and no friends because of his temperamental issues. In school, his teachers did not bother him too much; they were completely indifferent. If at all a teacher tried to interact with him, he would either snap at them or skip school for the next few weeks.

His teachers tried talking to his father, but he did not show any hope. Eventually, they decided to leave the child alone. He was academically inclined and did well in exams, so their job was done. No one really cared beyond that.

Raghav's father had failed to understand what he actually needed. He would buy things to make Raghav happy and when things did not lighten up the little boy, he would get irritated and scold Raghav. Eventually, Raghav grew up to believe that he was not meant for family life. Only a few lucky people enjoyed that privilege.

A few years later, Raghav grew up to be a handsome young man. As he grew older, he started dating a few women, but never felt any deep emotions for anyone. He found them either too confident or too dumb. Something or the other didn't work, and the relationship would not last more than a few months.

Ayesha was the only woman he had been with for over a year. In fact, she was the only one he could bear to be with. She was well-read and he found it easy to talk to her. She was sharp and intelligent. He would often seek her advice on important matters and she would help him come up with workable solutions.

Raghav believed in 'no strings attached' relationships. He had made it clear that he was a free man with no obligations, and would never be answerable for any actions.

Longing

It had been over a week since Raghav had seen Sushmita. It was evident that she was not one of the usual women he could win over easily. It was also unlike him that he could not get her out of his mind. Despite being busy with the launch and all the stress of the new project, he still kept thinking about her.

Initially, he was just curious about her. He kept wondering who she was and where she worked. He already knew where she stayed. It was an area predominantly for middle-class working professionals. Since that area was dotted with medium and large industries, many employees stayed there. She could easily be one of them.

Every detail about her kept playing in his mind. She was no extraordinary beauty, but she had a remarkable personality and a very pretty face. She was unfit and tired, and must have been boring too, for all he knew. Yet, there was something outstanding about her. She was alluring. Raghav could not understand why he kept thinking about her. But for him, she had become the most attractive woman he had ever met.

Such women did exist. Not in his world, but perhaps somewhere else. Women who were not just dignified, but also intelligent and humble. She was not like the ones he had met in the last few years. He was longing to see her again, to meet her, but didn't know how. She was probably married, since she had a child. She was possibly independent enough to not oblige to his riches, unattainable by virtues.

Barely a week later, he found himself taking the same route he disliked, just to have a glimpse of this strikingly attractive woman. He never dated married women, no matter how willing they were. They always brought emotional baggage, and led to a mess.

Single unmarried girls were hassle-free. He said to himself a few hundred times, "Oh no, not this one." Yet, he had to see only this one. Unfortunately, it was a Sunday and there was neither any school bus nor Sushmita.

The craving to see her again had increased, and he tried to reach the same spot again the next day at the same time. This time he did manage to see her, but only for a few minutes. Today, she had reached well within time and took only a short while to say goodbye to her child. He had waited hours to have those few minutes. Just a few minutes to capture her in his eyes. His mind was capturing each and every detail about her, including her wedding ring.

The more he saw her, the more he wanted her. Slowly his desires and hopes started increasing. He would try and reach the spot every other day. On most occasions, he would see her doing the same things. It had now been weeks, and the urge to see her had reached a different level. On days he would accidently miss catching a glimpse of her, he would be grumpy and irritable all day.

Helplessness

It had been two days since he last saw her. By now, Raghav was so involved in her that he had to see her every day. It had become a need. His compulsive behaviour would not let him be at peace. His restlessness knew no bounds. He had cancelled all his meetings. His body was shivering and his heart sank as his longing increased.

It was the same longing, the same helplessness he had felt as a child. The longing for love, the longing for care. Even after twenty-five-years, he had no control over his anxiety, over this longing.

He headed straight to his dad. He was in a very bad mood that day. He entered the house and did not say a word to his father, heading straight to his bedroom. He locked himself in, drinking and flipping through television channels. Initially his dad thought he was stressed at work, so he did not disturb him. But when he did not leave his room for hours, his father finally decided to ask him what was going on.

It did not take long for Raghav's father to sense that he had gone back to the same depression he had as a child. Back then, it had taken him years to really comprehend that his behaviour needed help. But now, he had been so careful with his child that he sensed it immediately.

The only fact that made it easy back then was, he could pick Raghav and take him to the doctors. But now he was too old to even attempt. He finally decided to just be by his side. He tried to support his son as much as he could. At night, he gave his son a tight hug, said nothing and walked away to his room. How he wished his wife had been alive! Raghav would have received all the love and care he deserved. She would have comforted him and helped him deal with all the challenges life threw at him.

By midnight, Raghav was too drunk to even care about Sushmita. It was only early in the morning that the longing struck again. It made him very impatient. He rushed out of the house just to make sure he didn't miss the school bus. Little did he realise that it being a long weekend, the school bus would not come.

Raghav was trembling from within. If he didn't see her today, he could do something dangerous. Something he may regret all his life. He had already spent the previous day drinking. He was determined to see her. There was no hope of seeing her that day, he knew, but he sat in his car for hours, just staring at the huge society gate, waiting for her to come out.

A few hours later, a black car drove out of the society gate and stopped near the temple. Windows rolled down And he saw her peeping out of the window. Beautiful curly hair made a mist around her face. Sushmita was praying and chanting, looking at the temple.

Her car stopped right in the middle of the road. It had blocked the road again, with another fleet of them honking again. A glimpse was enough to calm Raghav's anxiety though.

He drove off, smiling. 'Today is going to be a great day,' he thought. He wished everyone, right from the security guard, to his colleagues. He was cheerful and positive. How he wished each day was like this.

But at the back of his mind he knew he had to get this straight. He could never get her. He had to control his anxiety because she was unattainable. He could not depend on her for his well-being.

'Why me again?' he thought to himself. 'Why can't I get what I want? Why do I want something I can't get?' He knew he needed to see a doctor. He needed help.

It was probably the most difficult decision that Raghav had made that day. The first step was to admit that there was something wrong. And second, realising that it was beyond his control to take charge of the situation.

Initially Raghav was only reacting impulsively. Every time he wanted to see her, he would just keep waiting in his car outside her apartment. The action was more or less thoughtless, driven by uncontrolled emotions. As long as he would see her whenever he wanted, things were alright. But he did not realise that it was becoming an obsession. Only after the incidence of excessive drinking, he realised that the situation was much worse.

Nothing really helps

Raghav started having regular sessions with the same doctor who had treated him years ago to overcome his anxiety and depression. He was an old man who was extremely gentle and understanding. He knew Raghav from his teenage years and was well aware of the history. Knowing Raghav's strong ego, the doctor was extremely patient and gave him enough time to open up and share the truth about his condition.

After almost four sessions, Raghav finally started speaking. The doctor was the first person to know about Raghav's intense love that had turned into an obsession. The worst part was, Raghav loved someone who did not even know he existed.

The state when a person loves someone and has not been rejected but is sure of the rejection is extremely hurtful. The hope doesn't die, nor does it let you live.

The sessions with the psychiatrist were of very little use. They increased his confusion, and led him nowhere. He couldn't really change his condition, only control the intensity. He had fallen in love with a woman for the first time, but she was married to someone else and she didn't even know he existed.

She had no idea how strongly he felt for her. She was clueless about the fact that she had become his lifeline. She didn't notice that she was being followed every day, she had no clue that she was the reason someone lived. She was the oxygen for his life. Someone's feelings had grown so strong, that he could give up his own life for her. Only if she knew.

The doctor had now prescribed him anti-depressants that he had to carry with him at all times. At any point of time, if he felt that he was getting anxious, he was to pop two pills and immediately lie down, so his heartbeat could slow down. But the drug would only control the physical symptoms; the emotional unrest was still too deep to penetrate.

His condition had no cure, primarily because he never believed anyone. The doctor had warned him that if he did not take care of himself, he would suffer physically too. The doctor knew that he could only make suggestions, and Raghav wasn't the kind to listen. He was strong-headed and everyone felt helpless around him.

He never allowed anyone to influence him. He wasn't open to suggestions, and always refused to take advice. Apart from medication, Raghav was also advised to meditate. But he failed. He failed in pursuing anything. He knew he must follow the doctors' advice, but negativity had gripped his senses. Every time he tried to sit down for meditation, he would be left with no or very less energy and would finally give up.

Stalking

Every other day, Raghav would park his car near the society gate and wait for Sushmita to appear. Once he saw her, he would start his day. Once or twice the society watchman came up to his car and asked him about his reasons to wait there every day. He would always come up with some story.

At one such instance, Raghav got down from his car and actually initiated a conversation with the watchman. He had taken pictures of Sushmita in his phone. He showed them to the watchman and asked him all the details. The greedy man thought it was completely harmless and revealed some basic information. For a few thousands in his pocket, the watchman was more than willing to provide a detailed schedule of Sushmita. Though he did not know where she went every day, he did share everything else that Raghav wanted to know about her and her family.

It was now time to make some more progress. Next day, Raghav waited a little longer as per the details he was given. Sushmita dropped her son to the school bus. She went home and returned in her black sedan after close to two hours. This time Raghav followed her to her workplace.

With her full name and basic details with him, Raghav looked her up on social media. He also called a few contacts and got some more information about her and her family.

By now, Raghav knew everything about Sushmita. A minute to minute schedule confirmed that her only focus was her family and job. She hardly met anyone, apart from a few friends. She was a self-made woman, who had succeeded in the corporate world. She was happily married to a man named Sumit and had a 6-year-old son. She had no close family members and no history of affairs.

Raghav had become intensely obsessed with Sushmita. She was like a drug to him. Every time something unpleasant happened, he had to see her. Sometimes he would show up in front of her house, sometimes near her workplace, and sometimes, even at the vegetable vendor. He would go to great lengths to just get a glimpse of her face.

A strange meeting

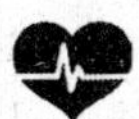

Sushmita had no idea she was being followed. She was so engrossed with balancing her life that there was no room for additional distractions. With passing time, her challenges at work had increased so much that she was oblivious to her surroundings. She never realised she was being followed

Expectations at her workplace had increased significantly after her last achievement. There were bigger challenges. The targets had been met. The quarter was nearing. She and her team had worked hard to meet the targets at the given deadline. The whooping profit of 25% was her big achievement of the year.

Her boss had flown in from New Jersey to review their performance. He was delighted to see the team doing so well within such a short period.

They all deserved a good treat. The young team members were already looking forward to the grand celebration they had earned for themselves. Like every year, this would be good, too. With only the close team members invited, everyone was at ease. The familiarity ensured everyone had a good time.

Sushmita, though, was not very keen. After the grand success of her second project, she still had some final things to tick out. She had been working late nights again, and was too tired to get dressed. But she had no option. Her teammates would feel bad. Mike, her boss, was in town, too. She had to go.

The party started off well at a nice cosy resort on the outskirts of the city. Though the place was not far from the city, it was lavish. Cosy interiors and well-lit lobbies gave the place a comfortable vibe. There were cosy lounges for separate parties, and a dance floor that gave the place a perfect blend of comfort and energy.

After a few drinks, the team started dancing to loud music. Food and drinks were being served and everyone was having the time of their lives.

Team members were cracking jokes and sharing stories. Mike, too, was enjoying the party with his team.

Sushmita had spent some time with the team, laughing her heart out. There were games to play and prizes to win. Sushmita participated in every game for a short time, but was bored after a while.

She helped herself with some mocktails, knowing that she had to drive back home alone. After a few drinks and a few starters, the dim lights made her very sleepy. The late nights she had been working since the last few weeks had drained all her energy.

She could not dance, so food was her only attraction. She was so tired that her eyes started closing on their own. She imagined her bed at home and craved to be in it soon.

She had to stay awake. Just to make sure she did not fall asleep, she quickly sneaked out into the nearby lounge. She found a large high chair and curled up to have a quick chat with Sumit.

After a long time, her phone rang and she woke up to find herself drooling in the chair, curled up in a wonderful-smelling jacket. Where was she? It took her a few minutes to gather herself and realise she was not alone. There was a good looking man sitting opposite her.

She quickly stood up, looked for her phone. There were around ten missed calls. She hurriedly called her colleagues to find them, but it was too late. They had already left. Her friend Riya had tried calling her, but she left when Sushmita didn't answer, assuming that she had left already.

Sushmita had left her car at the office, and arrived at the party with Riya. With no car of her own, she did not know how to go home. Cabs weren't safe in the middle of the night.

The cosy jacket still wrapped around her, she felt extremely embarrassed. She found out that the party happening in the banquet hall was cancelled. The man sitting in front of her had an unreadable expression. She shyly apologised to him and returned his jacket. She tried to talk to the gentleman, but he did not appear friendly. She asked him how they ended up in the lounge all alone. But he just smiled at her and gave her no great response. Sushmita understood that he had no intension to talk to her. She gave up the conversation, apologised for the inconvenience, excused herself, quickly grabbed her phone and called Sumit.

The resort was deserted at this hour. It was just Sushmita and Raghav. Raghav had not left her alone for her own safety. He wanted to talk to her, but this appeared so surreal. She was with him all alone and talking to him.

She was wrapped in his jacket as if she was wrapped in his arms, sleeping like a baby. She was carefree around him. She was close to him.

He decided to speak to her finally. So he went forward and introduced himself to her and asked her if she was okay, but before he could even utter a single word, she had excused herself and called someone. She also went away for a short while, possibly to freshen up. Raghav knew that the resort was closed. He followed her and kept waiting in the lobby for her to return. Sushmita took some time. Raghav, in the meanwhile, decided that he would drop her home, not knowing that she had already called her husband.

Sushmita walked out of the washroom with her hair tied up in a bun, the makeup washed off. She looked just like he had seen her on the first day. Before he could say anything, she thanked him and started walking away. Raghav started walking behind her, but soon, a tall, smart man arrived outside the resort door and Sushmita ran into his arms.

Raghav was speechless. Her expressions told him that she felt safe in Sumit's arms. Seeing her in someone else's arms broke his heart in a thousand pieces, each hurting and making his heart bleed.

"I dozed off, Sumit! How could I? Everyone left without me. Do you know how terrible I feel?" she cried.

"It's okay, sweetheart. I'm here now. Let's leave. You can sleep at home," he said naughtily, with a wink. She blushed as they walked away.

Raghav's heart sank with even the thought of someone touching her. How could he allow this to happen? She was his, and nobody else could have her. His blood boiled. He could only see the other man's arm around her waist. The man's strong grip around her bothered him. Every inch of her belonged to him, then how could she lean on tne shoulders of this man? How could she smile at him and how dare she blush at him? Just a few minutes ago, she was with him. How could things change so fast? His hands started trembling with pain. His heart was beating too fast and he started breathing heavily now. He pushed a few pills down his throat and waited for them to work. After numerous sessions with his psychiatrist, he had now learnt to identify the symptoms and immediately take medicines. Raghav could only see her face as he lay on the couch motionless.

That night, he had followed her to the party venue, when he saw her enter a car with a few young boys and girls. He did not want to take a chance with her being in danger, especially since there were other men in the car with her.

He followed the car to the resort and enquired at the reception about the party. Since it was an office party, he was the only outsider there. If asked, he would need a solid reason to be there. He quickly asked the manager to book a small banquet hall next to the party. If ever he had to reason his being there, he would say that he wanted invite a few people.

He paid for the hall and got in. It was a small room with huge curtains. The lights were not very bright, so it was a perfect way to stay hidden from others and keep a watch on her. He had found himself a comfortable high chair where he could see the entire party hall where Sushmita was. There was a huge glass wall between the two halls that gave him a complete view of the next room.

He kept a close eye on her and who she was surrounded by. Every time someone came close to her, he would get up and go closer to the glass wall. The fear that someone might touch her by mistake made him nervous. Sushmita had accidentally walked into the same hall where he sat to make some calls and fallen asleep. He felt so much better when she was around him, alone. There were no interruptions.

While Sushmita slept snuggling in the chair, her beautiful curly hair fell on her face. She looked like an angel. The bright green top she wore reflected on her face. He wanted to hold her tight and keep her in his arms. He wished the night would never end, so he could continue looking at her. He wanted to capture the picture in his eyes and heart forever.

He spent a few hours admiring her beauty, not disturbing her. A while later, her phone rang. She woke up and her husband took her away, and his worst fear came true. Someone else touched her.

Uncontrolled anger

Today he experienced the same feelings he had as a child. Back then, he would start throwing things around. He even hurt himself once when he saw his friend's mother pampering him outside school, just because he had performed well in a competition. Raghav had won the competition, yet no one had acknowledged his victory.

His driver had picked him up from school and when his nanny coldly asked him to change his clothes, without noticing the award, he had been furious.

He started screaming and throwing things all around. In the brawl, he threw glass all around and walked over the broken pieces. It hurt and bled, but Raghav kept walking on the glass. The nanny panicked and called his father. That was the first time his father realised how sour the situation had turned. His son needed immediate attention.

The anger and frustration had now recurred after the incident at the party with Sushmita, and Raghav took to alcohol. The sight of Sushmita with her husband had triggered strong emotions in him. His drinking increased and he didn't eat for days. For days together, he skipped work. He did not even open the door to his room for the house help. He locked himself in his room without any contact with the outside world. He kept looking at her picture. The image of Sushmita hugging and holding her husband would flood his mind and he would start drinking again.

Ayesha called him a few times, but he did not answer her calls. She began to worry, wondering what was wrong with Raghav. He had started acting very strange lately. He would not answer her calls, or return them. Even when he did show up to work, he wasn't his regular self. For the last few months, they had not spent any time alone and there was absolutely no communication between them.

Sometimes, Ayesha thought that Raghav had met someone new. When she asked around, she found out that he had not socialised in a while. He had not attended a single party. Her sources told her that he had arranged a party in some resort, but invited no one. She was told that he had spent the entire night in the resort sitting on a high chair. The staff had found it strange, but did not care too much since he had already paid them for everything.

Ayesha finally stopped bothering herself. She was an independent woman and she would not chase him too much, so she decided to leave him alone.

Taking control

When Raghav walked out of the shower one day, he saw himself in the mirror. He could barely recognise himself. He had lost a tremendous amount of weight, and looked much older than his age. Looking at himself, Raghav instantly decided to keep himself away from Sushmita. It had been a few months, and he knew that he had to accept the fact that she was happily married. He couldn't have her.

Things had become bitter, though. The more he avoided her, the more he longed for her. He stopped waiting for her and stopped following her. He did everything possible to stay away, but things did not improve. Not seeing her had taken a toll on his health. He was always irritated and tired. He would have muscle pain in his arms every now and then and a constant urge to drink. The symptoms of depression were now showing physically. He knew he could not afford to continue like this.

He was no longer the helpless child. He was successful enough to win anyone over. Something had to be done. He just could not figure out what.

He finally decided to confront her, meet her and make himself irresistible, so she would leave her husband and fall in love with him. He started spiralling into a whirlpool of madness, imagining and thinking the impossible. His mind was possibly tired of the negativity, so it started healing itself. He came to a point where he started getting positive thoughts. He started thinking that she would become his. No marriage is perfect, and no one can be perfectly happy with someone. He had seen enough couples to know that there were loopholes in every relationship. He just needed patience to find out the cracks in her marriage, so he could manipulate her.

Being in her vicinity would be the only option to win her over. He had stalked her for days, physically and virtually. He knew the trend of her activities. Her office timings, her regular visits to the market, the salon she visited, and her child's school. He had details about everything.

He would also keep a tab on her social media accounts frequently about all the new posts she added and liked. He would check accounts of her friends to find out what they were up to. Most of her posts were about latest news, relationship quotes and pictures with her husband, or with her son. There was hardly any picture of her alone. He started analysing her social media posts to find out more about her. In each picture, she stood very close to her husband.

The pictures told a hundred stories about her love for her husband. Their smiles, their closeness was disturbing, pictures clearly proved that this was not going to be easy. These two were very much in love with each other.

Separating her from her husband was not going to be an easy game. The twinkle in her eyes while she was with him spoke about the immense love she had for him. In some pictures, they were dancing or smiling at each other. Her social media had pictures of their home, their new car and many memories she had with her husband. He was not worried about the child. He could easily accommodate him in their life later. Her husband was the only problem.

He had tried all means to find her mobile number. He even got her social media account hacked. All her pictures were now with him, close to his heart. He could see her whenever he wanted to. At least it was some reprieve. He especially liked the one in which she was tagged by her colleague. The picture was taken during the party. Sushmita was wearing a green blouse with black trousers. It was the night that he had finally got to be with her for some time. It was also the same night that had left him heartbroken.

Raghav had made a detailed list of her friends, and tried to identify the close ones. Who were her colleagues, and the people she usually interacted with? He thought of all possible options before he came up with a plan.

He would soon meet her, befriend her, and make her fall in love with him. Then, he would separate her from her husband. That way, no harm would be done. It would appear that it was her wish, and he had not played any role in her decision.

Next, he had to concentrate on the new project. The last few months had been so bad that he had barely been able to concentrate. He would walk into the office like a zombie, drink coffee all day, and walk straight to the bar when he got home.

By the end of the day, there was only coffee and alcohol in his body. He had drowned himself in negativity, and he had to get things straight. He had wasted so much time and had almost killed himself. This had to stop immediately and he was now determined to take control of his life. He had to achieve the two most important goals of his life – marry Sushmita, and complete the resort. The later was in his control, so he decided to focus on the project and bring it to completion.

The first thing he did the next morning was to hit the gym. He worked on regaining the muscles he had built over the last few years. Once he was pumped up, he got dressed and walked to the office. His breakfast meeting with his father had to wait for yet another week.

He scheduled a management meet to discuss the progress of the project. This project was his dream. He could not deceive that. After getting all the details, he discussed the next steps. Detailed planning was done and deadlines were set. The whole team was now committed to give their best and make this project another big success.

Soon, the action plan was made. The team quickly started working on the financial plans to create a proposal for the investors, and presentations for his travel partners in Europe and America.

After weeks of planning and analysis, the data was ready. He was prepared to travel to the US to present it to his investors. Each and every little detail was verified to ensure that there were no loopholes in his plan.

The investors had been in the business for a long time. Raghav had worked with them earlier, and their suggestions had helped him make his previous project a great success. He was able to return their money within a few years with good profits. This time too he was sure that they had faith in him, but they would not risk their money if the project was not planned well.

He was scheduled to travel the next month. He had taken this time to review the proposal and check if he had not left anything unattended, as their rejection would cost him too much.

After month-long hard work, it was finally time to meet the investors. Despite all the preparations, there was something amiss.

In spite of keeping himself occupied with work, Sushmita did not leave his thoughts. He would start and end his day with her picture. Raghav kept thinking that if he could meet her once, he would be able to convince the investors – a superstition that he had built. He knew that he had promised himself to control his emotions, but he could not resist. He had started believing that she was his lucky charm.

He had planned it all – how he would meet her, what situation he needed to create so that it appeared to be a coincidence. The very thought of meeting her had made him feel positive. If he was successful, he would be set for life. She was the woman who could give him all the happiness in the world.

Raghav had become so obsessed with the thought of marrying her that he had stopped being reasonable. He did not realise that this obsession could also turn things the wrong way. He was convinced that he was doing the right thing and there were no *what ifs* in his mind.

He always thought he was right. The fact that he had fallen in love with a married woman was justified in his eyes, because love is blind. Her loving her husband was justified, because she did not know that there was a man better than him. He always found a reason to justify all his actions. He had created his own questions and his own reasons too.

He changed his definitions of right and wrong as per his convenience. Destiny taking his mother away, and having a loveless childhood was wrong, and now he had the right to compensate the same in his own way.

Sumit

Sumit was a charmer, someone who always wore a smile, no matter what. With cute dimples, he looked adorable, just like a grown-up kid. He worked in the finance sector and would often spend long hours in the office. Everyone in his office admired him for his temperament and the way he handled relationships. A tall, good-looking man who was always calm – no wonder he was popular amongst his female colleagues the most.

He respected them, and would extend his support whenever possible. Sushmita knew about her husband's popularity, and would often tease him. There was unquestionable trust and unconditional love between them. She would always wink and joke about his female colleagues and how she was lucky to have him as her husband.

Sushmita and Sumit had met each other during an internship in a small company. Sushmita was a developer and Sumit was a financial analyst. They both came from middle class families and the first job meant a lot to them. They would spend long hours working in the office.

Sumit always offered to drop Sushmita home when they worked long hours, and soon, they became friends and fell in love with each other.

They had begun their life together, and soon, with hard work and dedication, they both succeeded in their respective careers. They bought their first house together, and created memories of their own, followed by all other milestones.

They had a small world built on trust, love and hard work. Their happiness revolved around each other. They found happiness in small things – cooking together, watching movies, and grabbing a cup of coffee late at night.

After Amey was born, their love had grown by leaps and bounds. They were good parents, and did everything possible to raise a good child. They were so compatible with each other that each knew when the other was stressed, and often helped each other. The two were inseparable, and over time, their likes and dislikes had also got in sync with each other. Though they were different personalities, they knew each other's shortcomings very well. Even when they fought over small things, they never went to bed in a bad mood. Sumit being such a loving and caring husband would always patch up and would give her a long hug. He knew that life was hectic and mundane, and took every effort to lighten up the family mood. Love and respect were the foundation of this happy family.

Pretty pink

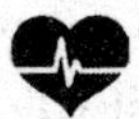

It was already December. This time of the year was lovely. People slowed down. Sushmita's team in the US had started leaving for long vacations. Work pressure was low. There were no urgent meetings. Her last delivery was over, and the new project was yet to start. People around were in a holiday mood, waiting for Christmas. Most of them were planning vacations and overall the atmosphere was pleasant.

Back home, Sumit was also relaxed. He too had completed all the work for the year, and the atmosphere in his office was light. He would come home early and spend time with Amey.

Sushmita was in a very good mood today. Tonight, she was going to go out for dinner with Sumit and Amey. Sumit and Amey were going to pick her up from her office, and they were to go to a new Chinese restaurant.

She was so busy during the year, that she barely got time for herself. She rarely dressed up. There was never enough time, so she always compromised. Today, though, she decided to give herself some extra time to get dressed. It had been ages since she spent time on herself.

She pulled out a baby pink top and a pencil skirt. Since she had gained some weight after her pregnancy, she never wore clothes that would make her look fat. But today she tried on her well-fitted skirt. She put on make-up, and a perfume that Sumit had gifted her. It made her feel attractive, a feel good factor that was much needed.

Dressing up once in a while did well to her soul too; it made her feel confident. She was really looking forward to get over with work and enjoy the family dinner.

Seeing her walk out of the house, Sumit's eyes shone. "What's so special, Mrs Rai? Who do you plan to kill today?" he said, as he pulled her into a tight hug. "You look great, sweetheart. You should give yourself some time more often."

"I will, Sumit. I certainly will. I just need to manage my time a little better," she replied. Giving him a quick peck and leaving lipstick marks on Sumit's face, she gave him a tight hug. "Wait for the magic tonight," she whispered in his ears and stepped out doing a short happy dance.

When Sushmita entered the office, the compliments started coming in right from the elevator – from her subordinates, to her office friends.

Just as she logged into her system, she got a call from an unknown number. Thinking it would be a telemarketing ad, she ignored it. The phone rang again. This time, she answered it just to avoid repeated calls.

A deep voice spoke from the other end. "Hello ma'am, this is your financial advisor from ICDB bank. This is regarding your investments and portfolio overview. We have been asked to meet you in person to discuss this further. With your permission I would like to have a short meeting with you."

"Sorry, I am at work," she said. Just then, it struck her that her policy was ending soon, and she needed a renewal. Instead of going to the bank, she could tell this person to do it. After a long pause, she agreed to meet him at a coffee shop near her office.

During her lunch break, Sushmita went to the coffee shop, but did not see anyone. She quickly called the number, but it was out of reach. After trying a few times, she got annoyed and decided to leave.

Just then, a tall man with a deep voice said, "Hi there!" It was the same man she'd fallen asleep in front of, on the day of the office party.

"Oh, hey! We've met before, right?" she said, a little flustered.

"Yes, my jacket still has stains," he said with a grin.

"Oops, correct. I'm so sorry for that day. I'm not a party person and I was so tired, I just dozed off. I cannot apologise enough," she said apologetically.

"You can, actually. Care for a coffee?"

Sushmita smiled. With her dimples and the pink top, she looked like a cute doll.

God was sending him signs. She was probably dressed for him. She looked like an angel straight from heaven sent by the Almighty to cure all his pains and worries. He wanted to hold her in his arms and kiss her. But he had to hold back. This was not the right time.

She took a long pause and finally said, "Thank you so much for the invitation, but I'm swamped with work. I wouldn't mind a coffee, but I have a few commitments in the office. Sorry, again."After a brief goodbye, she walked away.

Raghav was mesmerised by her presence so close. She had politely rejected his offer without insulting him, that is what he liked about her. She did not insult him, but still did what she felt appropriate. He was not surprised by her response, but definitely flabbergasted by her beauty. The pink blouse with those delicate earrings made him want her like never before. Her curves made her so desirable. The spark in her eyes was like that of a child.

There was no way she would have coffee with a stranger like him. His job was done, and his desire to meet her before he left for the US was fulfilled. He could take care of other things when he returned.

The tussle continues

On arrival in New York, Raghav checked into a hotel, had a hot shower and headed straight to the bed. The travel was well-planned. The hotel was not far from his client's location. The meetings were scheduled from 10 a.m. the very next day.

After a good night's sleep, he woke up early to have a quick glance through his work, and make sure he was ready for the meeting. Just before he moved towards the office building, he quickly glanced at Sushmita's picture. "No one can love you more than I do, my lucky charm," he said to the picture in his phone and walked into the office with a grin.

It was now almost evening. All the meetings scheduled for the day were over and he now had the whole evening for himself. He took a cab and reached the city centre to grab a bite and look around. Dinner was anyway not on the agenda.

During his solo stride, he blankly kept looking at the designer shops. He came across so many beautiful things. How he wished he could have Sushmita by his side as his wife. He imagined her asking him to buy her all the things women usually demand. He had money to buy them, but no one to demand it from him. No one would get upset if he refused. He missed her. He grabbed a sandwich and sat on a nearby bench. Being away from the mundane routine did him good. He was relaxed and could clear his mind.

It was already 8 p.m. and it had started getting lonely. He picked up his bag and started walking towards his hotel. Just then, he crossed a few designer stores and set his eyes on a beautiful diamond and emerald necklace. 'It would look great on her,' he thought to himself, but only if she allowed him to gift it. He gave up hope, and walked away to the hotel. It did not make any sense to buy such expensive gifts if they were never going to be accepted.

The next day, he had the most important meeting of the trip – a final meeting with the managing committee with all the directors and important stakeholders.

By now, the plan was on his fingertips. He could tell the figures without looking at the presentation. He walked into the board room a little before everyone else, to be sure that he did not miss anything. He checked the projector, had a quick glance at the meeting room to ensure that it was enough to accommodate everyone.

After all the pleasantries, the meeting started on a very positive note. The questions that came from the board members all indicated positive responses from their end.

Raghav looked like a Greek god in his light blue business suit. His confident demeanour spoke volumes about his involvement in the project. The presentation too was made very carefully, with all the required details mapped in graphs and images to give a clear understanding.

However, the managing director, Ronald, seemed to have doubts.

"Mr Mehta, there is a discrepancy in your figures. Have you checked them yourself?" he asked.

That came as a surprise to Raghav. He had been so sure about the plan. How could this happen?

Raghav calmly requested Ronald to elaborate. Ronald took a short pause and resumed, "Raghav, you have a fantastic proposal and anyone other than me would have approved this plan. But you have missed some important elements in your financial planning. You will have to reconsider it. I will not tell you what, but I give you three weeks.

You can send me the new plan within this time period, and if you nail it, consider the deal done. Else, please excuse me." Saying this, he walked out of the room, leaving Raghav disheartened.

Raghav waited a little longer to run through whatever he was told. But he just could not get it. He called his finance head to quickly start reviewing the proposal. The entire team would have to re-evaluate all the details of the plan.

Disheartened, he left the office early and headed straight to the hotel. He desperately needed lunch, and a quick nap. There was very little that he could do from the US. He could not take control of things until he reached back home.

That evening, he stepped out of the hotel. The weather was pleasant, and he thought having a stroll in the city would do him good. He came across the same diamond and emerald neckpiece while walking. Brushing his thoughts away, he walked into a café and called a few friends to catch up later that night at a nearby pub.

He knew that if not anyone else, Riya would show up. She had a huge crush on him and every time he was there, she was more than happy to meet him. At this point, he needed someone else. Some new company and Riya were the perfect choice. They knew each other since a long time. As he had anticipated, later that evening, Riya reached the pub. Raghav was already having his drink.

She looked stunning; sexier since they last met. Raghav greeted her with a tight hug and whispered into her ear. The alcohol had already started affecting him. After a few dances, the pub started getting very loud. Raghav and Riya left the pub and headed straight to his hotel.

The alcohol, the music and the beautiful weather had done magic. Raghav pushed Riya against the lobby wall and kissed her passionately. By the time they reached the hotel room, they could barely keep their hands off each other. Raghav's lips moved from her face to her neck, and explored her even further. He was different today, more passionate, more longing. Riya was shocked to see this version of him. She enjoyed every bit until it lasted.

Misery

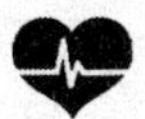

The next day, Raghav's flight was in the afternoon. Raghav had the whole morning to himself. Riya had left early that morning. He did not stop her. He just wanted to be alone.

Nervousness had hit him again. Seeing Riya sleeping next to him in bed that morning had aroused guilt. Was it because of the meeting or was it because of something else? Had he failed in the project? Had he betrayed Sushmita? How could he have missed something on the project plan? What exactly had gone wrong? How could he sleep with another woman? His body, his soul belonged to Sushmita. Being intimate with another woman was betrayal and he felt guilty. Thoughts poured in torrentially. They burnt him like wild fire consuming all his senses. He walked in to the shower wishing there was a way to clean out the previous night.

Riya's face kept flashing in front of his eyes. He could imagine Sushmita being angry and hurt because he had cheated on her. In the beginning, he told himself that he was delusional.

Sushmita was not there. She did not love him. There was nothing between them for him to feel guilty about, but everything he did to Riya kept coming back. The guilt kept hammering his brain. Everything hurt him.

He could hear himself apologising to Sushmita. The shower area was now filled with steam. Sushmita started pulling away from him. He tried to hold her, but could not. The walls started getting closer, pushing him away from her. Sandwiching him between them. He could not move his body. Maybe all the oxygen in the room was over too. The walls had now reached him. He was stuck between them. He called for help but no one could hear him. Did any sound come out? The lights started getting dimmer till there was a complete black out.

Raghav found himself lying on the floor in the shower. It must have been a while since he was lying there, completely helpless, soaked in sweat. He somehow managed to get back to the room and popped his pill. He lay on the bed, wondering what was happening to him. He started counting numbers till the medicine kicked off in his blood, calming him down.

Post breakfast, he headed straight to the jewellery store. He knew in his heart that the neckpiece belonged to her, and he would make sure she wears it. He was determined this time, sure of what he wanted. His project would be successful and she would be his wife. He just had to focus more. Believe more. He had been good for a long time, giving himself excuses to stay away. Nothing seemed to work. Another nervous breakdown was the last thing he wanted. He would die if she did not marry him. His life was meaningless without her. He had to be selfish and snatch her from the other man.

The countdown had begun. Three weeks for the project, and a few more for the wedding. Sometimes, the mind plays its own games. Once the mind is exhausted, it starts freeing itself of all the worries. It refuses to take any more stress. That is the point when it starts believing that all the desires are achievable. It starts making the person believe that it is happening for real. It is the mind's own survival mechanism to believe that all the desires are coming true and everything you dreamt of is actually happening around you. Raghav's mind had already reached that stage. His stress levels had already reached the threshold. Since he could no longer bear the pain, his mind started believing that Sushmita was already married to him. He was at a stage where there was no distinction between real and unreal. What the mind wanted was real, what the mind did not want was not.

Raghav bought the necklace and some more exquisite things for Sushmita, determined to gift them to her on all their special occasions – one on the day of their wedding, one on their first night after, one on the first anniversary. Their wedding would be a grand affair, where all the who's who would be present to bless them. She would look so beautiful in her red lehenga. He could picture himself performing the marriage rituals, making their relationship legitimate, legal and socially acceptable. All this had already become a reality in his mind.

Sushmita was not a woman he would want to have a casual affair with. She was not a woman he wanted to just date and leave. She was to stay forever and ever. He would also adopt her son. He must be a darling, too. He would love him and care for him just like his father would. That would make her happy.

He would refurbish the house for both of them. Their son would have a lovely room for himself. She would get all the luxuries she deserved. His dreams had no end. The planning had no end, but it made him happy. So what if it was only in thoughts? He could turn his dreams into reality. He had read that if you want something from the bottom of your heart, one day you would get it. This is all he wanted.

Action

Despite the jet lag, Raghav had not slept all night. He had been thinking about his next steps. He wrote down his plan in his planner. He scanned through his mobile contact list to find what and who can help him overcome his issues.

He messaged one of his school friends and asked him to meet immediately. Raghav sat at the café, waiting for his friend Chirag. He had been working with a multinational bank, and had made it big. Chirag was the only person who had remained his friend despite all the behavioural problems Raghav had during his growing years. Not once had Chirag complained, or expected anything different. He stood by Raghav through all his difficult times. They sometime went months without talking, but were always just a call away in times of need.

Chirag knew something was wrong. He hoped Raghav wasn't going through depression again. Chirag's doubts were confirmed as soon as he saw Raghav. His otherwise good-looking friend looked much older, all of a sudden. He looked unkempt and disoriented.

He decided to hear him out.

Raghav looked awful and he knew it. But at least he would be able to speak his mind today. After thinking for a couple of hours the previous night, he had concluded that the current team lacked certain skills. He needed another member who would critically access the project plan and rectify it. The new member would head the finance team and would sort out the mess. His current team had been working for a week, with very little success. He was losing time and he could not afford that.

Raghav spoke to Chirag about all that was happening in his business. He told him how his investors had given him a very short time to clear the loopholes in the proposal and how his existing team was unable to find the problem. Raghav told Chirag that he needed someone with a fresh mind to join his team and study his proposal and rectify it. He briefed Chirag on the skills he was looking for in the new Finance manager. Chirag quickly browsed through his contacts and came across a name – Sumit Rai. Yes, he was the guy. He was an extremely intelligent and hard working guy who could bring Raghav out of the mess. The issue was, however, to get him to join the company. Sumit was very risk averse, and would not change his existing job for this new emerging company.

Sumit Rai's recommendation from Chirag was no surprise. Raghav had information about Sumit; rather he had first read everything about Sumit and adjusted his requirement as per Sumit's profile. Coincidently from the professional network site, he knew that Chirag had connections with Sumit. His plan was to get Chirag to lead to this name, and make it appear like a coincidence. That is how he would get introduced to Sushmita also. If things went bad later, he would have a solid cover. He would always have a story to narrate and proof that Raghav was not intentionally building contacts with Sushmita.

Sumit was doing well in his company. He was always the go-getter and had earned a good reputation because of his intelligence and hard work. One day, he got a call from a recruitment company for the position of vice president Finance. The position sounded extremely lucrative, but when Sumit looked up more information, he found out that it was a new venture. Though the company's performance was incredible, Sumit's response was negative. He could not risk his job. He had a family to take care of. Though his wife was earning too, they had financial commitments. Changing his job at this point was not a good idea.

That evening, he discussed it with Sushmita and they decided to reject the offer and continue with the existing one. This job offered him stability as well as flexibility. It had become his comfort zone and he was not ready to leave it. Certainly not for a new company.

However, later during the week, things took an abrupt turn. All his meetings were cancelled. Over the next two days, all his assignments were taken back from him. He was no longer on the mailing list. He was not informed about important matters, and his boss had started to behave hostile towards him.

He was surprised. He kept wondering what must have gone wrong. He thought hard, but found no answer. Finally, he decided to wait and watch. This was a very difficult time for him.

The insecurity and uncertainty made him nervous. He would often call Sushmita and discuss the issue with her. She would comfort him and assure him that things would work out. There were times when he made multiple calls to her just to vent out his frustration. She would calmly and patiently handle all his mood swings because she knew he needed her support during these testing times.

Two days later, his director invited him for a meeting in his cabin. Such an abrupt one-on-one meeting with the director was surprising. Sumit was told that his position had become redundant and he would either have to relocate to Chennai or quit his job. He was given two days to respond.

Relocation to Chennai was out of question for him. He could not leave his wife and child alone in this city. They both did not have a family to support them who would stay with Sushmita while he was away. Quitting the job was not an option either. He had financial commitments. It would be a total financial disaster, but at least he could stay with his family. He would stay home for a few days and look for another job.

He called up Sushmita and told her what happened. She was shocked too; the whole situation was difficult to digest. For the many years that he had served the company, Sumit was also a very valuable employee. How could things change suddenly? Just like Sumit, she too was not ready to stay alone in the city with a child. If Sumit would quit, her salary would not be enough for all the expenses they had.

Both felt totally helpless. The idea of losing a job terrified them. He knew that he had to earn a certain amount of money to maintain the lifestyle they were used to. They had savings, but they could not live off them.

Sushmita and Sumit spent hours exploring all the possibilities. Both spent the next two days in tremendous stress. When all the options seemed difficult, they finally decided that Sumit would quit and call the recruitment agency that had called him a few days ago. They were not sure whether the job was still available. Little did they know that it was the beginning of a very dangerous game.

The plan was working exactly as Raghav wanted. Sumit was supposed to join the new office today. Raghav was not usually available for new recruits, but this was a special case. Sumit was his only means to reach both his goals. Raghav personally welcomed him and ensured that he was comfortable. Sumit was given a cosy cabin right next to Raghav's. After a brief introduction, Sumit was given details of the current situation. It was made very clear to him that he had to work with tight deadlines.

Things started moving quickly in the office. Sumit would spend hours in the office, sometimes late at night, doing the analysis. Often, Raghav would drop him home, in the hope of meeting Sushmita. There was something about Sumit. It was very difficult to not like him. Very soon, he became popular in the office. Everyone seemed to like working with him, including Raghav. He was a humble and polite man, composed and chivalrous. He could make anyone comfortable.

Gradually, Raghav started getting fond of Sumit too. 'Why did he marry Sushmita?' he thought. Had she not been involved, they would have been great friends.

In any case, Sumit would be the one who would suffer, no matter what. It would be difficult for him to lose her. But someone had to lose so the other could win.

The three-week period had now come to an end and the fresh proposal was ready. New figures were calculated and a much more detailed plan was made. Raghav and Sumit were to fly to the US to make the final presentation. All the necessary arrangements were made. Sumit was to back Raghav up, just in case he needed assistance. They were set to achieve their biggest goal.

Raghav waited impatiently at the airport. Sumit insisted that he came on his own, since his wife wanted to see him off. Sumit had asked Sushmita to not bother herself, but she wouldn't agree. She was going to miss him terribly. Sumit had never travelled alone for work. They always travelled together and most of the times, it would be vacations. The thought of not seeing him every day was disturbing, but it was a matter of a few days and Sumit had to do this.

For no rhyme or reason, Raghav reached the airport much earlier than the scheduled time. There was no reason for him to get so impatient. They had ample time to catch the flight. His impatience, though, was to see her. This time he did not need to do something special. His plan had worked well so far.

The jet black car appeared at the airport. Sumit quickly got out of the car. Raghav was already nervous. He waited in the lounge area just next to the entry so he could have a good view of Sushmita and Sumit.

Just then, Sushmita got out of the car too, wearing a plain

white shirt tucked into her figure-hugging blue jeans. She wore no make-up or jewellery other than a pair of white pearls in her ears, displaying sheer confidence and grace. Her aura was so positive that Raghav needed no more affirmation that this trip would be successful. She quickly got down and helped Sumit with his luggage. She hugged him tight. By the time Raghav could walk up to her, she was shooed away by the traffic controller.

Achievement

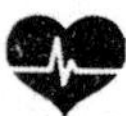

The meeting in the US went very well. The presentation was successful and the contract for the investment was signed. The new plan was more realistic and had consideration of all the minute details. This time Raghav and Sumit could show the investors their profit projections. This was the biggest milestone for Raghav. He had no words to thank Sumit for his dedication and intelligence. What his entire team could not do in such a long time, he had done just in just a few days. No wonder Sushmita was glued to him. She knew her husband's worth.

After the meeting, Raghav showed Sumit around and would occasionally strike conversations about his family. Those few days were enough for him to get a complete understanding of how his family was set. These little details would later help him in his planning. He was still gathering information. He wanted to get every possible detail that would lead him to her.

Initially, he tried to find cracks in their relationship. He tried to convince Sumit that he too could date a few women, and need not be so loyal to his wife. Sumit, however, was so staunch, he would just smile and say nothing. During one such instance, Raghav introduced Sumit to a lovely lady he knew. Sumit politely refused, and walked back alone to the hotel. Raghav was shocked. He now wanted to know what kept him so bound to her. Had it been any other man, he would not have been able to refuse such a beautiful woman. There was something more to it that he had to find out. Or was Sumit in the same phase as Raghav? Even when there was prettier girl available, they both wanted only Sushmita.

Once they reached India, the entire office was thrilled to hear about the success of their deal. This certainly called for a party. Immediately, a success party was planned. For the next few days, the young team members only discussed the venue and date and clothes and food. No one seemed to be interested in working. They had already logged in too many long hours before the presentation and everyone wanted a break. This was a good opportunity to create a happier atmosphere in the office.

Sumit, too, decided to leave work early for a few days, to make up for all the extra hours he had spent in the office. Sushmita was heavily overloaded, since she was managing everything single-handedly. She needed a break too. She was tired and irritated managing the office, home and Amey all by herself, but she never ever complained about her stress. Sumit had been noticing it too, but he was helpless. Now that he was relaxed with the office work, he decided to give her a little break. That weekend was her birthday. She deserved a treat – maybe a dinner at a fancy restaurant. Nothing pleased her more than a candle light dinner so he too planned to send her on a shopping trip so she could pamper herself and he would take care of Amey in the meanwhile.

Unfortunately, the party was also planned the same day as Sushmita's birthday. He would not be able to spend a lot of time with her alone. Sushmita did not mind that too much, though. It had been a long time since they were married. They had spent many birthdays alone and would be spending many more to come.

Sushmita was not fussy about such things. She was mature, and very accommodating. The day of the party, she wore a blue silk saree, with statement earrings to accentuate her looks. A bare neck and bare hands would create a focus on her radiant skin.

She looked like a proud wife and a happy mother. She was Sumit's brand ambassador for today. She was peaceful and calm, making a mark for herself with her own identity and did not need any external validation. Being a wife and a mother was one dimension of her being, and today, she wanted to live that. Her family was a big part of her success and she wanted to flaunt it.

Just as they reached the party venue, Sumit got a call from his colleague to discuss an important issue that had come up. He told Sushmita to go ahead and that he would join her later. Sushmita was annoyed at this, though. It was his party and she did not know anyone there. She wanted to enter the venue with him, and now he had gotten caught in a call.

Raghav welcomed her in the hotel lobby. Of course, she had met him before. It was such a small world, she thought as she exchanged pleasantries. They both agreed to what a small world it was that they had met thrice at different occasions in such a short duration. Sushmita was happy to meet Raghav as her husband's boss and was happy to be a part of Sumit's professional group.

Raghav whole-heartedly complimented her on how stunning she looked. For a brief moment, Sushmita felt uncomfortable. She thought about what a coincidence it was that she kept bumping into the same man at different places. Of all the people in the world, the same man is her husband's boss, too. A woman's sixth sense is God's gift to her. It is the most powerful weapon she is equipped with. It sends warning and alarms her about the possible danger, but only if she chooses to use it. Unfortunately, Sushmita did not choose it then. Instead, she brushed her thoughts aside, thinking he was just being polite, and convinced herself she was thinking too much.

He accompanied her in the elevator, ensuring that no one else entered it while they were inside. For a few moments, he wanted to be with her, alone. In just a few seconds, he would have to share her with the world. It was her birthday, and she had to be with him.

As she entered the party hall, she was taken aback. The hall was pitch dark all the lights were switched off. A spotlight shone directly on her. She was surprised, but thought all guests were welcomed like this.

Raghav escorted her to the centre of the hall, where a huge birthday cake was waiting. He handed her the knife and made her cut it, whispering birthday wishes in her ears. He fed her the first bite. All this happened so suddenly that Sushmita could not register what was happening.

Sumit was nowhere to be seen. She was sure that he had planned it for her. He could have been around while the cake was being cut, though. She assumed he was taking pictures. That's what he always did. She brushed her thoughts away and thanked Raghav for such a wonderful surprise.

Just then, Sumit walked in. It was a big surprise for him too, but Sushmita thanked him and he did not want to disappoint her by saying that he had not done it. Perhaps Pooja had planned it all. Pooja was his executive assistant and one of the chirpiest women in the office. She was the youngest team member and was always looking forward to celebrations. Maybe he had mentioned it to her and she had decided to plan this. He did not recollect having mentioned it to her, though. He did not think too much about this and decided to thank her later in the office. He was sure that she was the only one who would come up with such an idea. Not once did it occur to him that there could be someone else involved and this could be a hint to a bigger problem.

Small things were giving big clues to both Sushmita and Sumit, but they did not notice them. We all hear about strange things happening around us, but we never think they can happen to us, too. Sushmita's discomfort was her sixth sense telling her to be careful. Only if Sumit and Sushmita would have spoken a little about the surprise, they would have easily understood that something was not right.

Raghav took the centre stage and thanked Sumit and team for their wonderful job. The party started with loud music, and very soon the young team hit the dance floor. Sumit was the first to be on the floor. He loved to dance, and enjoyed every bit of it. He knew Sushmita would not join him so he did not even ask her. It was an unsaid rule between them. When they were in social gatherings, they did not spend time together. They would talk to new people and enjoy the function just the way they wanted it.

Sushmita tried to talk to a few people, but soon headed towards the dinner counter. She was famished, as always. Sumit could take as much time as he wanted. She was also a little bored because she hardly knew anyone. "Planning to cuddle up in a cosy corner?" she heard Raghav ask with a naughty smile.

"Well, I actually don't mind. But I don't want to be left alone today," Sushmita replied with a twinkle in her eye. "You know how embarrassed I was that day. Please don't bring it up again," she joked. With that, they started a conversation. The topics would drift from economics to politics to personal choices to latest technologies. She was so easy to talk to. Intelligent and so clear with her thoughts. He was deprived of meeting such women. He was left to the mercy of dumb but good looking women who were only good at seducing men. Even on that front, Sushmita could easily beat them. Her smile did to a man what bare skin could not.

A step ahead

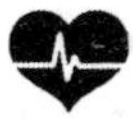

Soon Sumit, Sushmita and Raghav became friends. They started spending more time together. Sumit's house became Raghav's second home. Sushmita cooked for them, often. She made coffee for their late night discussions, and sometimes left Amey with them and caught up with her personal time. Amey, too, had become fond of Raghav. Raghav had taught him to solve the Rubik's cube and they went hiking regularly. It was a sad twist of fate. Raghav had started growing fond of the family, but at the end of the day, it was not his family. He was still a guest. It was Sumit's.

Sushmita still held Sumit's hand. He still pulled her closer to him. She did not ask him how he wanted his coffee, she just knew. There were many small things that gave Raghav a feeling that Sushmita was not his. When they went shopping, she only asked Sumit for his opinion. She would only ask Sumit for his opinion and Raghav would often feel left out. On one such occasion, they had gone shopping, and Sushmita wanted to buy a new saree for Diwali. She picked out a few and draped them.

Every time she draped a saree, she asked Sumit how she looked, but did not ask for Raghav's opinion.

She looked great in blue, but Sumit loved orange, and she eventually bought the orange one. Raghav did not mention which one he liked. She did not ask him, but only if she had looked at him once, he would have told her how beautiful she looked.

The colour was brilliant, and she looked like a goddess with her divine beauty. Something about her was so peaceful. She could make a man feel safe and secure with her reassuring personality.

The next day, Raghav reached the same mall and bought the saree he had liked for her. This was his gift. He would preserve it and give it to her on the right occasions, even if they were not easy to create.

On Diwali, Raghav was invited to Sumit's house. A few other friends were also invited. Their house was beautifully decorated and the puja brought in a holy feeling. The dinner was traditional, cooked by Sushmita herself. Raghav reached when not many guests had arrived. By now, he had become quite comfortable with the family. He helped himself to some water since the two were busy.

Just then, the doorbell rang. Sushmita opened the door, and was overjoyed to see her college friend, Akash. Before she could even welcome him, he gave her a tight hug.

"Oh my princess, my first love, that scoundrel Sumit stole you from me. You look so hot in that saree!" he joked.

Sushmita blushed and asked him to keep quiet. Akash walked in and punched Sumit, teasing him. "You rascal, you took my love from me."

Sumit pulled Sushmita close and playfully said, "I know she is beautiful, but she is mine, and always will be. Now just shut up and join the party."

As everyone was enjoying the moment, a few glasses broke in the living room. They all rushed out to find Raghav bleeding profusely and pieces of glass lying around him. No one knew what exactly happened. Just then, Sushmita ran to get the first-aid box. She pulled Raghav towards the kitchen sink to wash his hand. She did it so forcefully, that he had no choice but to follow. She washed his hand and dressed his wound, just like she would do to Amey.

All that while, Raghav just kept looking at her, not saying a word. The way she held his hand made him forget the pain. Sumit joined them with a glass of water for Raghav.

"All well with you? What happened? Did you fall?" Sushmita asked, thinking that something was wrong with him.

In spite of her asking so many questions, he did not utter a single word. He just kept looking at her. He wanted to hug her. And tell her that he couldn't tolerate anyone touching her. He could not accept that a stranger had hugged her. No one in the world had the right to do that. She was his and only his. No one could touch her and she shouldn't blush for anyone else. He hated Aakash and he hated Sumit. He would kill if anyone tried to touch her. He wanted to take her with him to his house and keep her safe, away from the world, safe in his arms. Her touch would heal him from all the wounds life had given him. She would fill his life with all the love that he had been deprived of. She would care for him just like she had done today. Love would fill their lives.

Today, he had an anxiety attack again, but had not taken the medicine to calm down. Sushmita's touch had done wonders. Today, she made sure that he ate well and paid special attention to him. She was so kind.

For her, Raghav was a good friend who needed attention because he had hurt himself. There was nothing beyond it. Had it been anyone else, she would have behaved the same way. That is what friends are for. She failed to realise that even her kindness would send wrong messages.

Today was a special day for Raghav. It was the first time that she had touched him. The feel of her hands, the aggression of her grip, the worry in her eyes, her hair, and her fragrance – everything about her was so sensual. He had been smiling ever since he left their home. Today he wanted her all for himself, closer to him. Today, his lips wanted to feel her, his hands craved for her skin. Today, he did not want to be in his senses. The chances had become bright for him. Soon, she would be in his arms, and he would feel every inch of her. Love her, caress her and fill her life with so much love that she would forget her past, forget her husband.

Sushmita had always been a motherly person. She was a mother to Amey and wife to Sumit, who she often mothered too. Care came to her naturally, ever since childhood. The incident with Raghav was not out of the blue. She was a little worried about Raghav. She had sensed something strange in him today, but she could not understand what it was. She mentioned this to Sumit that night, but he dismissed the topic, saying that she thought too much. Sushmita too left her thoughts at that. It had been a tiring day and she wanted to give herself some rest.

She just cuddled Sumit and laid her head on his shoulders. Sumit pulled her closer to him and gently massaged her aching feet. It was bliss to have a husband like Sumit. Sushmita was feeling so relaxed with the massage. She kissed Sumit for all the love and care he had for her, and minutes later she was fast asleep on the couch. Sumit gently picked her up in his arms and carried her to the bedroom. He covered her with a warm blanket and finally called it a day.

The feeling of unease, though, did not leave her. She would sense strange vibes when Raghav would be around. There was no doubt that he was an amazing person, yet there was something weird about him.

The project had picked up with all the funds being transferred to Raghav. The final plans were made, government approvals were happening and the construction work had started.

During this time, Raghav and Sumit travelled to visit the site to check the progress. During their journey, they would have long conversations. Raghav often tried to initiate discussions about Sushmita. He would enquire if she was doing well with the hope to hear more about her, but Sumit would often cut the topic short, since he did not like to discuss his family.

During one such visit, Sumit appeared a little distressed and mentioned that Sushmita was unwell and he needed to return home soon after the visit. He would not go the office since there was no one to look after her. They had sent Amey to school and Sushmita was alone. Raghav tried to ask some more questions, but Sumit just mentioned that she was down with fever. The thought of Sushmita being unwell and alone at home made him very uneasy. He wanted to see her immediately, but it was a little too late. They were already on their way and now making an excuse to return would make it obvious.

After a few minutes, Raghav asked the driver to stop the car. He pretended to have gotten a call and stepped out. After coming back, he asked the driver to turn around and head back. Sumit was surprised, but Raghav convinced him that he was urgently required in the office for income tax related work. They agreed that Sumit would go to office and deal with the income tax officers, while Raghav visited his father who was unwell.

Sumit reached the office and tried to find out what the officers were looking for. He was given vague replies, both from the office and from Raghav himself. That meant he had to first spend time to find out what was to be done, and then work on it. That would take hours. He didn't mind it, because he knew he would reach home sooner then he would have if he had to complete the site visit. He spent about an hour just to find out the issue Raghav was talking about, since no one knew exactly what was happening.

After a while, Raghav called him saying that he was close to Sumit's house. He asked if he should check on Sushmita, and see if she needed anything. Sumit was busy in figuring out the problem, additional help at the home front was certainly welcomed, so he agreed instantly.

When Raghav reached home, Amey was not around. He rang the bell but no one opened it for some time. He did not have the keys either; he rang the bell again and waited patiently for Sushmita to get up.

Sushmita could barely open the door. Her face was pale with fever. She was so weak, she could barely stand. Raghav helped her to the bedroom and made some tea. He called Sumit after a good half hour and told him to come back home and take her to the doctor.

He wanted to do it himself, but did not want to take a risk. He was extremely cautious about his actions. While with her alone, he did everything possible to take care of her. He told her that he had already called Sumit and he would be on the way, when in reality he had not called for a long time. Sushmita had no sense of time. The medicines had made her drowsy. She fell asleep immediately after finishing her cup of tea, assuming that her husband would be home soon, and Raghav would stay only for a few minutes.

When Sumit arrived, Raghav pretended to be sitting in the living room. However, Raghav had been sitting in the bedroom right next to her all through, staring at her.

Covering up

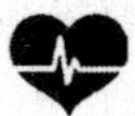

Life had taken a complete U-turn for Raghav ever since he had met her. He had not met Ayesha since then. She had called him a few times, but he had ignored her. Today, she had called him early in the morning to wish him for his birthday. She insisted that they met in the evening to celebrate. Of course, Raghav was now in a fix. He wanted to celebrate his birthday with Sushmita, but could not say no to Ayesha too. So he finally decided to invite everyone for dinner.

Raghav was an opportunist who would make something out of this dinner too. Today, he had to meet both women together and fulfil his agenda.

For the past few days, especially after the Diwali party, he had sensed that Sushmita had started getting hints about his intentions. His feelings for her were so intense, that being oblivious was impossible. That day he had also made a big mistake; all the while he had kept looking at her with such intensity, it was unlikely that Sushmita had not realised it.

If she ever found out, she would start distancing herself from him. To be sure that this does not happen, he decided to remove her doubts. He decided to introduce Ayesha to Sumit and Sushmita as his girlfriend, so Sushmita wouldn't doubt his intentions.

That evening, Ayesha met him at his house. She looked ravishing. Her figure looked as though it had been moulded to fit perfection. Her face looked like an artist had painted it. What else could a man ask for?

Raghav and Ayesha reached the restaurant before Sumit and Sushmita. They were waiting in the hotel lobby to receive their guests. As soon as Sumit's car entered the driveway, Amey ran to hug Raghav. They were always happy to meet each other. Raghav carried the child and walked towards Sumit to welcome him. Raghav asked Sumit about Sushmita's whereabouts before he could even greet him. The thought of not meeting her on his birthday was disturbing.

Just then, Sushmita walked into the hotel wearing a beautiful white silk salwar kameez with a red dupatta. Her earrings glittered, and their reflection was falling on her face. The kohl made her eyes lively, as if they were dreaming a thousand dreams about him. Her lips accentuated with the red lipstick looked like a rose, waiting to tell him how much she loved him.

Sushmita shook hands with him as she wished him. He held her hand a little longer. She noticed it and tried to slip away. He quickly gathered his thoughts and realised what he had done. Immediately, Raghav introduced Ayesha as his girlfriend and the love of his life. He spoke such great things about Ayesha that it gave an impression that he was madly in love with her.

At the restaurant, he could not take his eyes off Sushmita. By now, Sushmita had started getting a strange feeling about

Raghav, especially the way he looked at her. But he claimed that he was in love with Ayesha, so it was safe to conclude that her doubts were baseless. She felt relieved that her instinct was wrong. She was pleased to meet Ayesha. She was both intelligent and beautiful. Ayesha had a pleasing personality, and both Sumit and Sushmita liked her.

The dinner was interesting, with great conversations and amazing food. After dinner, Raghav and Ayesha headed back to his house. The dinner was not included in the plan, but Ayesha was happy to meet the Rai family. They were interesting and it seemed that Raghav was happy spending time with them.

Ayesha had arranged for Raghav's house to be decorated. She had planned a candle light dinner, but since Raghav wanted to introduce her to his friends, she did not refuse. Raghav was pleasantly surprised to see his house adorned with flowers and candles. It took him seconds to realise what was coming.

It had been a long time since he had been so close to anyone. The incident in the US had been very traumatic, and he did not want to repeat it. This time, however, he could not stop himself. Just because it happened once, did not mean it would happen again. Ayesha was irresistible, and her presence could drive any man crazy.

He pulled her closer and kissed her gently. This was not the first time Ayesha was getting intimate with Raghav, but Raghav was different today. She had never seen him so passionate before. At first she thought he had missed her, but as his grip started getting harsh, she felt the panic rise. He got fierce. His hold became strong, and he didn't let her go. It felt like he was scared of losing her. The passion turned into insecurity. He started murmuring, "Please don't leave me. I will love you more than him. Trust me, no one will ever love you more. He is not good enough for you. You are mine, I cannot let you go."

On hearing this, Ayesha almost choked. "Raghav, who are you talking about? Leave me, what is wrong with you?"

But he did not loosen his grip. Finally, Ayesha had to push him away. Raghav came back to his senses after the push and realised he had made a huge mistake. He had spilled the beans. He had offended Ayesha and given her too many clues. He had to handle her well. Fortunately, he had not mentioned Sushmita's name, at least that is what he hoped. He felt terrible from inside, confused and scared about the repercussions his actions would have.

Ayesha left, without saying a word. She did not need an explanation or clarification. She knew exactly what was wrong. The next day, she sent her resignation letter.

Tainted

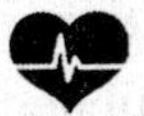

Misery had struck him again. What he had done to Ayesha could not be excused. He had never insulted a woman before. The guilt was killing him. He thought he had stooped so low that he could not forgive himself. It was four in the morning and he was sitting in his living room, drinking. His brain could burst anytime now.

His thoughts were like wild fire. They were running in all directions, turning everything to ashes. All his confidence, his hopes were dead. He did not want the sun to rise; he did not want his solitude to end. It was his solitude that gave him freedom to think. No one had control over his thoughts and he could believe that Sushmita was his. He could imagine her the way he wanted. There were no rules or boundaries.

His phone kept ringing. His father had been calling him for an hour. He had promised his dad that he would visit him but had completely forgotten. The alcohol had made him lose any sense of time. When Raghav did not answer, his father called his driver. He had already sensed that Raghav was up to something.

Mahashankar Mehta had decided to confront his son now. He decided to take hold of his child's life. He could not see his son fail after all the effort he had made to build a good life for himself.

On entering the large house, he could see Raghav all alone in deep sleep. The empty bottles lying around the table told the story of what must have happened. He looked closely, without waking Raghav up, to get a better idea. He found exactly what he was looking for – a picture of a woman in a pink top. He took some more time to observe the picture and realized that this picture must have been taken without her knowledge, because she was not looking at the camera. Her attention seemed to be elsewhere. He kept the picture to himself, and tried to wake him up after some time.

Raghav had been woken up with so much love after ages. It could not have been anyone but his father.

"What are you doing here, dad? Is everything okay? Why didn't you call me? I would have come to see you," Raghav asked.

"We already had plans, but you did not come. I called you a few times, but you did not respond. Anyway, I made breakfast for you. Freshen up, I'm starving," he said.

Raghav quickly got up and went to his room. When he returned, his dad was picking up the empty bottles. He felt ashamed of himself. He had scared the old man and shattered his hopes.

At the breakfast table, Raghav's father questioned him about what was bothering him. Raghav refused to talk, saying it was nothing but a few business issues. His father saw through the blatant lie. "I want to know the truth, every bit of it."

Raghav knew he could not lie anymore. He tried to avoid the conversation, but the old man kept looking at him with such emotions that Raghav poured his heart out. "I love her dad, I love her too much. I can't live without her, but she is already married, and she will never leave her husband for me. She does not even like me. I know, no matter what I do, she will never be mine."

With this, Raghav collapsed on the table, sobbing.

His father felt terrible, but decided that he would not give up. He could not let his son break.

He gave him a pat on his back and took him back to the living room. When Raghav had stopped crying, his father asked him more questions. He knew his son had a psychological disorder and treating him was next to impossible. When he learnt that Raghav had already spoken to his doctor about his obsession with Sushmita and it had not helped, he became really worried. Nonetheless, he decided to accompany his son for another session.

The next day, his father arrived again with a large suitcase. He had decided to move in with Raghav and did not care what Raghav thought. He had to be with his son to make sure that he did not collapse again. When Raghav had taken over the business, they had decided that they would not stay together and so Raghav had bought a new house for his own privacy. The circumstances, however, were different now. It had become risky to leave Raghav alone. He had become depressed and his father feared that he had become suicidal too.

Things had become a little better with his dad moving in with him. At least there was some company during dinner. But the guilt of petrifying his father was still killing Raghav. It had shaken him from within. The problem was no longer personal. It had become a family issue. Something had to be done soon.

End of a happy family

Raghav was fed up with his situation. He could not wait any longer to make his next move. He would certainly not continue this way. He decided to visit a hill station alone to plan his next move. He had to get rid of Sumit now. That was the only option left. With Sumit around, Sushmita would never be his.

Breaking their marriage was extremely difficult, so there was no other option left. He had to make a good plan and it had to be flawless.

In two days, Raghav chalked out a plan. He had made a mind map of all the aspects that he had to consider and kept revising it. He kept revising it until it was perfect. He evaluated all the possible risks – his father was the only one who knew about his feelings for Sushmita, but he posed no danger.

He should not have printed that picture of Sushmita. That way, his father would never have seen it. He had no idea that his father might come and visit him. He printed the picture because he wanted to feel her presence around him. He had taken pictures of her on different occasions while he used to stalk her. He got them printed in far off cities so that even the photo studios could not recognize either of them.

Raghav was not emotionally prepared to hurt Sumit, even though the plan was in place. He kept struggling with his thoughts. On one hand, he wanted Sushmita; but on the other hand, he could not kill Sumit. The emotional outbreak was intense. A whirlwind of thoughts captivated him day and night. His work started suffering again, along with his health.

Raghav was not a bad person. His obsession and his failure to control his feelings had led him to make such drastic plans.

Raghav was now waiting for an opportunity. Even after all the thoughts he had in his mind, he was confident that what he was doing was the right thing. Days were passing by and the pretence of being a good friend continued. He also made sure to not give any further clues to Sushmita.

After their last meeting with Ayesha, her doubts were probably gone. He had been observing her behaviour too. After the meeting, she had become friendlier, assuming that it was safe to be with him. She had also asked about Ayesha, and Raghav easily convinced her how much he loved her.

It had now been over a month since Raghav was waiting for an opportunity to execute his plan. But nothing seemed to be working. Finally, Raghav approached Sumit and reminded him that it was time for the next site visit. Sumit confirmed that he would visit the site the following Friday. Sumit reached home and mentioned his site visit plan to Sushmita. He would be gone for a night and would reach the next day.

The next three days were horrific for Raghav. Though he had all the contacts required for this job, he had never used them. He had never hurt anyone before, but everything was fair in love and war. Later that evening, he made a call. This plan would certainly cost him a fortune, but it was all worth it.

At 5:30 a.m. on Friday, the black Creta hit the express highway. The main highway was crowded, but as soon as Sumit took the diversion towards the site, the roads started getting emptier. The road went through a small village with little traffic. The radio played loud music, but Sumit kept driving at his steady pace. The road was narrow. A little distraction would throw him straight into the valley. He usually travelled with the office driver, but the driver had called in sick.

As he took a sharp turn, a truck came at a high speed from the opposite direction. Truck drivers usually drove slowly on these tracks, but this one was probably inexperienced. Sumit tried to move his vehicle to the right, but there was hardly any space. Before he could even decide his next move, the driver banged his truck into the car. The car crashed against the mountains, crushing the vehicle, breaking the glasses and killing the future of one happy family.

Raghav got a call from an unknown number. The man on the phone said, "The job is done, sir. The man won't survive. I don't know about the wife and child." Raghav was astounded.

As per the plan, Raghav was in the vicinity of the accident.

He rushed to the spot. He had no idea that Sushmita and Amey were there. It was an official tour and Sumit was to travel alone. Raghav's heart was racing. He had to see her. He had to see the little one. He was trembling with fear.

He had already called the ambulance. On reaching the accident spot, all he could see was the three of them in a pool of blood, with the doors locked. Sumit's head was on the steering wheel. He was not moving. Amey was sitting next to him. Sushmita was bleeding profusely. From the outside, he could not tell who was alive.

Raghav was drained after looking at Sushmita. He sat on the side of the road, feeling completely helpless. He wondered if the universe was playing a joke on him. Soon, a few villagers came to help him. They broke open the window and opened the doors. By now, the ambulance had arrived. Raghav, without a second thought, pulled Sushmita out of the car and rushed her to the ambulance. Sumit and Amey were declared dead immediately, but Sushmita was still breathing. Her heartbeat was slowing down with every second. Raghav called another ambulance to take the bodies to the city.

The thirty-minute drive to the hospital felt like a million years. Her pulse was dropping, she was unconscious, and bleeding profusely. Sushmita and Raghav were both struggling for life in that moment. Every breath she took was a ray of hope for him. Every heartbeat was an assurance. Every cell in his body was focused on her. His heart was aching with the guilt of what he had done. Why did it never occur to him that something like this could ever happen?

Thursday night, while having their meal, Sumit had mentioned that he would be away for a night for the site visit.

Monday was a holiday for Amey, and Sushmita had taken a day off from work. When Sumit mentioned that he was going on a short trip, Sushmita suggested that they accompany him. After his work was done, they could travel to a nearby resort and spend the weekend there. It would have been a short family trip.

Sumit had not told Raghav about the changed plan as it was an impromptu decision and seemed irrelevant. He had thought he could call him later and give him a heads up that he would not be available over the weekend.

Pray and hope

On reaching the hospital, Sushmita was rushed to the operation theatre. Her condition was fragile and she was at great risk. The chances of her survival were little, and she might remain vegetative her entire life, even if she survived. Severe emotional trauma was another thing that she would have to deal with. In such cases, patients hardly have any desire to live. This all contributes to slowing down their recuperation.

The operation was over, but Sushmita was still in coma. The doctor called Raghav to discuss Sushmita's condition and further course of action.

"Usually patients with a strong will power recuperate faster. In this case, the will power is a very important factor especially because the woman has lost her child and husband. It is extremely difficult to determine what impact this accident has done on her. Post operation, Sushmita would need psychiatric treatment. During this time, she may get suicidal and would need tremendous care. You have to be very careful. She is very fragile and how her body and mind would react cannot be predicted."

Dr Raj was a very straightforward man. He wanted Raghav to have a clear picture of what it meant to be with such a patient. The trauma of losing your child and husband in a car accident would leave her scarred for life. At this point, it was difficult to guess what was hurt the most, her body or her mind.

Sushmita had to go through a blood transfusion because of heavy blood loss. Two hours later, she was brought to the ICU. She was on ventilator and had tubes running all through her body.

The doctor informed Raghav that the next three hours were very crucial for her. If she did not regain consciousness, she may have to undergo another surgery. Raghav had collected all his strength to face this situation. He had to own up to it now. This was his doing and he could not get weak now. His mind demanded that his body remained strong. His psychological issues had no place right now. She was dependent on him and he had to be strong for her. The mind is very tricky. During all these events, not once had Raghav felt breathless or lost control. He stood there like a lion to protect his world.

Sushmita regained consciousness within those three hours. Her first word was "Amey" – very unclear, but very strong. She was assured that he was safe with his dad. Raghav had to buy some time for her to recuperate. He knew someday he would have to tell her the truth, but he wanted some time. He was not sure if she would be able to handle it so soon. She was bedridden for more than two weeks. The recuperation was slow but steady.

The hospital had become Raghav's second home in this time. Not once had he gone home or left her alone. He would eat in the hospital canteen and would sleep on the small extra bed the room had. His body ached because the bed was too small for his large frame. He had not eaten properly after the incident. Nightmares haunted him and pain refused to leave his body.

On the day of discharge from the hospital, Raghav did not know where to take Sushmita. If Raghav took her to Sumit's house, she would be at a risk of more mental trauma. If he took her to his, then it would lead to much bigger questions. Raghav finally took her to his father's house. He already knew about her and he would not ask too many questions. He requested his father for help and he happily agreed to move back to his own place with Sushmita.

Sushmita was shocked to find out that Raghav had not taken her to her own house. All the while, she wanted to meet Sumit and Amey, and today, when finally the day had arrived to meet them, he was taking her somewhere else.

Every time she enquired about Sumit and Amey, she was told that Sumit was injured too and could not leave the house to meet her in the hospital. Children were not allowed anyway. While in the hospital, she understood the situation and never argued about this.

When they reached home from the hospital, she asked Raghav why she was brought to such a strange place. Raghav assured her that it was his father's house and the doctors had requested him to keep her away from the two because her wounds had led to a lot of complications. The infection had become contagious and Amey would be at risk, since he too was in bad health.

He asked her to stay patient for a day or two and that soon, he would arrange something. Sushmita had no choice but to believe Raghav, the only person she could trust right now.

Sushmita settled down in Raghav's father's house. Nursing care was arranged for her. Raghav and his father had moved in, but since the house was so huge, she had all the privacy she needed.

The medicines were strong and kept her drowsy. For most part of the day, she would keep sleeping in the room. She could barely stay awake for a few hours. After the tenth day, when her dosage was over, she regained her full senses. Raghav now had no cover. He had to tell her the truth.

Shattered

One evening, Raghav asked her to get dressed, and he said they would go out in the fresh air for a while. A table was arranged in the garden under a tree. It was his favourite place when he was growing up in this house. Raghav's father volunteered to join them for dinner, in case he needed support.

It was a lovely evening. The candles and yellow light had created a beautiful ambience. Sushmita impatiently waited to meet Sumit and Amey. She was really looking forward to this dinner. It had been a long time since she was in the hospital, and this was a good change.

She wanted to hug her child today, but at the same time, was scared that her haste would put their lives in danger. She got ready, put on clean washed clothes, tried to look decent, and reached the garden. For Raghav, it was such a relief to see her walking. She had lost a lot of weight and her skin was pale. She had bags under her eyes. But her heart was beating, she was alive and she was with him, which was all that mattered. In the last couple of days, Raghav was constantly doubtful about her health, he was in constant fear of losing her. He had hoped and prayed that she would be healthy again

The evening began with small talk. He formally introduced her to his father. Though they had been staying in the same house, she hardly left the room to know that there was someone else in the house too. She whole-heartedly thanked them for taking such good care of her and allowing her to stay in their house during the difficult time.

Sushmita tried hard to focus on the conversation, but could not really do it. Her eyes were wondering, waiting eagerly for Amey and Sumit. How her hands longed to hold her Amey. There had not been a single day when she had not held him. She was so used to being around with him all the time. Her whole world revolved around him. Though she longed to meet Sumit, her longing for her son was much more intense. Thoughts about her son always kept her distracted. She would often think about him, his well-being and his school.

She did not want to appear impolite in front of Raghav's father, so she tried to concentrate on what he was saying, but after a while, she burst out saying, "Sumit and Amey are coming, right?"

Raghav remained silent.

"I will leave with them, Raghav. My bag is already packed. I am grateful to you for letting me stay here, but I miss my home. I would like to go back. It's difficult for me to sleep without my child. I have to see him, first thing in the morning. I hope you understand. I am so used to being around Sumit and Amey, I feel terribly lonely without them."

Raghav slowly got up and sat next to Sushmita. He was now holding her hand. Sushmita got nervous. "What is it, Raghav? I don't have a good feeling about this. I am going home. I will remain in my bedroom. I will not touch Amey, but at least I will be able to see him. I know I am not well and I could get them sick too. But staying away from home is worse. This way, I'll never get better. My son and my husband mean the world to me. Especially after the accident, we need each other. We need to be alone. I am terrified of what Amey must be going through. He is in pain, and his mother isn't with him. I don't want him to presume the worst."

Raghav patiently heard her out. And finally said, "Sushmita, you will never be able to see Amey or Sumit again. The accident was so bad, they could not make it. I am really sorry."

Sushmita was speechless. It took her a while to be able to speak again."This is not true, right? All this while, you've been telling me that they are coming to meet me, and now you are saying they are dead?"

"I am not lying, please believe me. I did everything I could, but the crash was massive. Only you survived, and your chances were also weak. You have undergone a major surgery. There was little chance of survival. We were actually prepared for another surgery. Please trust me, you had immense blood loss. Despite all the treatment, your wounds did not heal; rather, it got infected. A separate treatment was started for that. I had to make up stories to buy time. If I would have told you earlier, you would not have ever healed. I would have lost you, too. The situation was not appropriate to reveal the truth. It had to wait till you were ready to take it. It was difficult for me to see you in pain and hiding things from you. I know all this is a lot to take, but we don't have a lot of options. Your recuperation is the only focus now. Slowly, we will figure things out. I cannot leave you alone in this situation. I have been advised that by the doctors."

Sushmita kept staring at Raghav, without saying a word. She didn't shed a single tear. She left the table and went to her room. Raghav tried to stop her, but his father asked him to wait. "Let her cry. She needs to process this. She needs her solitude. She is a strong woman; she will handle herself".

Deep dark hole

Sushmita lay on the bed, staring at the ceiling, for hours. She did not cry. Raghav was nervous by now. He knew that if she did not vent out her feelings, it could be dangerous for her. He kept calling her name, but there was no response. He knocked and requested her to open the door. He was scared that she might do something to herself. His heart started beating faster, the sheer fear of what she might do to herself brought tears in his eyes.

What had he done! Why did he even start this? Why did he meet her? Why did he fall in love with her? Why was he so obsessed with her? Why such a devilish act! What if she never spoke to him again? The flames of thoughts were burning him from deep inside.

She did not open the door, no matter how many times Raghav knocked. The doctors had already warned him about the possible emotional danger, and the possible psychological problems she would go through, but it was actually happening now.

Raghav tried to kick open the door, but the door was very strong. There was no way he could open it. Finally, he had to call a carpenter and force his way into the room.

She lay on the bed, unmoving. Fortunately, there were no signs of anything dangerous, the first thing he checked was whether she was still breathing. Though she was breathing, she lay lifeless. Something had happened to her during those couple of hours.

She was a completely different person. Her eyes were dead. There were no emotions in them. They had disappeared in thin air. No happiness, sadness, or life. There was an endless void. The colour on her face ran out. Sushmita was now a mask, with a beautiful lifeless face. She was unreadable and impenetrable. Raghav tried to talk to her, but she did not give any response. He contemplated that his voice was not reaching her. Raghav wondered whether she had even heard him, or registered his presence.

The doctor arrived in the middle of the night. He simply gave her a sleeping pill. "She needs to switch off her mind. She cannot cry because the shock is so intense. Let her sleep, and meet me tomorrow morning," he advised.

The psychiatric treatment had already begun. The doctor advised to rekindle memories that would stir up some emotions inside. Raghav took her to Sumit's house to collect her belongings. Sushmita did not cry. She had stopped eating or reacting. She was just breathing. When they reached the apartment, she just touched the name plate and entered. Raghav did not wait for her. He just went to the bedroom, opened her wardrobe and collected a few essentials. All that time, Sushmita sat on the couch like a stranger. Raghav carried the things out and drove back home with Sushmita by his side.

He did not know what was happening to her. He thought she would react after going to her house, but she still did not. She behaved as if it never belonged to her.

Quite some time had passed. The doctors had prescribed anti-depressants, but they made no difference. She would just keep sleeping and when she would be awake, she would not talk; she would just keep starting at nothing. If the nurse tried to feed her, she did not eat. She stared into nothingness for hours on end. She had started to look like a skeleton – a lifeless body.

Raghav did not lose his cool during this phase. He spent time with her every day. She only listened to him and ate only if he fed her. Raghav cared for her like she was a child. He had to take care of all the little things. As per the doctor's advice, he showed her a few pictures she had taken with her family. It seemed like they had had a lot of fun. But none of it helped. She remained as it is. It had been three months, and she had barely spoken.

Raghav decided to visit another doctor. He wanted a second opinion. Dr Shyam Sundar was an experienced doctor. He prescribed a different treatment after studying Sushmita's history in detail. But the medicines made no change; they were not helping Sushmita. They would just put her to sleep for long hours. There was no sign of improvement.

Finally, Raghav took Sushmita to the doctor again. He changed her medicines again. Some more tests were done, and her illness was diagnosed. She was diagnosed with selective amnesia. Certain parts of her memory were completely lost. She had lost her sense of being. She could hear everything, but could not relate. That's why she did not react.

The chance of her getting her memory back was low. The doctor advised Raghav to take her to a different place. Staying in the same city would only aggravate her condition. She needed serious medical help, both for her mind and body. Her mind was like a deep well with no end of thoughts, one after the other, confusing her about what is the present and what is the past. The time had come when she could not understand whether what is going on is real or just her mind making it up. Once she was healthier, she could travel.

The medicines given after this diagnosis were quite effective. Sushmita had started responding to the situations around her, with at least yes and no. She understood what was happening around her. Her food intake was gradually increasing. But she had not cried, nor had she ever asked about Sumit and Amey. Though it was worrisome, the doctors advised Raghav to not pay attention to that aspect for a while. Once her physical health improved, she would also start reacting. Patients of selective amnesia usually recall specific memories – especially the positive ones. They misremember negative life events. This seemed to be beneficial for short term, but would need treatment in the long run.

Raghav just wanted to have some more time at his disposal. His first priority was her health. The memory loss was going to take time, he knew.

❖

Three months later, Sushmita had come back to normal physical health. She was looking healthier and her skin was glowing again. She was better oriented and tried to keep herself engaged, sometimes with gardening, other times, cooking. She would cook for the three of them. Raghav knew that cooking was her passion and did not stop her. His father, too, had started enjoying her company. Most evenings, the old man would sit and chat with her in the garden. Sometimes, they watched movies together. She had become like his long lost daughter. Raghav was happy to have her around. The house was desperately in need of a woman like her. Cooking had given Sushmita a way of keeping herself busy. She would cook 4-5 meals a day and would insist that everyone ate it. Raghav could no longer have his egg white and protein shakes. There was always rich Indian food. Sometimes, Raghav got annoyed because he was gaining too much weight. But his father would enjoy all the delicacies she made.

The garden around the house had started blooming. Sushmita and Raghav's father had planted some trees, and the house looked beautiful. The traces of her memory loss were still very evident. At times, she would frantically clean every corner of the house, even repeatedly. There were times she would clean the same place several times, thinking she had not cleaned it before. Sometimes she would cook lunch 2-3 times. But no one objected. The house staff secretly joked about it, but would quickly stop with a pitiful statement.

Though her physical health was recuperating, the revelation of Amey and Sumit's death had taken her mind into a dark tunnel. The grief kept pushing her down so far into the darkness, that she had no memory of her past life. The grief of losing her child was so intense, that it had shattered her entire being.

Sushmita's psychological condition was deteriorating day by day. Memories of her past life were fading rapidly. Sometimes, she remembered fragments of events, but would fail to understand them because they were incomplete. They would flash randomly, leaving her confused and helpless.

She would do things and wondered how she knew how to do them. She would try and recall, but there was no memory. Her confused mind would make her lethargic, and she would continue sitting in the same position for hours, till someone in the house would notice it and bring her back to her senses. She also often forgot what she was doing and why she was doing it at all. Raghav was calmly waiting, for the times to change. For better days.

Light peeking in

One day, Raghav asked her if she would like to join him for his official tour to Paris. He had been there before and thought she would like the place. Sushmita did not know how to react, but the thought of going out with Raghav secretly pleased her.

She had slowly regained her strength. Slowly and steadily, she had started living her life. Though there was no clear orientation, things had improved for her.

It had been a few days since she had started to notice him. How she landed up in this house was still a big question for her. When she had asked him, he mentioned that she was his friend and had lost her family in an accident. He had not given too many details, and she had believed him. She had no reason to doubt him, after all that he had done for her.

She was so happy here. Everyone around was so good to her. Though she spent most of her time alone, she enjoyed the company of the wise old man. Raghav met her at dinner sometimes, because he usually came home late, when she was asleep. Ever since she had regained her senses, Raghav had started spending less time with her and was now concentrating on the project. He would call his dad and ask about her, but never made obvious to her how much he loved her as he did not want to trigger new emotions.

However, Sushmita did notice the small things he did for her. Her first coffee of the day was always served to her exactly the way she liked it. Her favourite cookies were always in the kitchen. Her room always had a vase full of her favourite flowers. The ways his eyes shone when she wore pink. She often wondered who had got her that dress. She could not recollect buying it herself. Every time she wore it, Raghav would complement her. He looked happier. She didn't know if she was imagining it, but yes, she had noticed the things he did for her.

Raghav and Sushmita reached the Charles De Gaulle airport. She saw extremely beautiful buildings on the way to the hotel and fell in love with the place instantly. It had changed her mood, but they were too tired to explore the city the same evening. They checked in at the Saint James. The hotel was an architectural wonder. It almost defied definition. The rooms were so beautifully done, it was a dream come true for Sushmita. Raghav had been to Paris before, but had never booked such an expensive hotel. He had spent a fortune for this place, but he wanted the best for Sushmita. Though this was much above his budget, he decided to splurge. These were going to be the best days of his life.

Sushmita had become a totally different person in Paris. She would dress up every single day and try to look her best. She was enjoying every bit of it. Their long walks down the Champs-Élysées, their visit to the Montmartre or the Arc de Triomphe, everything was so special. Her favourite was the city tours in the open bus. They had done these bus tours so many times that Raghav finally got bored of it, but Sushmita would always insist on the bus tour because it gave her an open view of the city. They had been to every part of the city, had visited every museum and garden. Sushmita enjoyed the fresh air, and the light vacation mood of the tourists around the city.

It was the last day of their tour. They stayed in all day, and planned a tour of Paris at night. Sushmita was really looking forward to this tour. She had read that Paris looked extremely beautiful at night and was eagerly waiting to see the beauty. She wore her red off-shoulder dress with golden heels. She wanted to look her best today and make this tour a memory for a lifetime.

During her visits to the psychiatrist, she had tried to recall her past and had failed miserably. She had broken down, unable to join the jigsaw puzzle of her life. The doctor had finally stopped trying his method. Instead, he advised her to create new memories rather than remembering old ones.

The journey so far had been terrible for her. She would remember her old life just in bits and pieces. She remembered working in a multinational company. She remembered where she stayed. She could remember her childhood, and her early profession. But everything related to Sumit and Amey was wiped out. She did not even remember having met Raghav in her earlier life. She believed him because he asked her to.

She had now decided to accept her physiological state and not challenge it anymore. She had decided to accept the fact that she would not remember anything from the past and rather create new memories that she could remember in the future.

When she entered the hotel lobby, Raghav's heart skipped a beat. She looked gorgeous. Her beauty was a delight to his eyes and her virtue had delighted his soul. He had no words to describe her. Her beauty was something he wanted to capture in his eyes and let it sink into his heart. While his heart wanted to drown in love, his eyes still wanted to cling to the shore. His eyes spoke a thousand words, if only she could read them. If only she felt the depth of his love. Love is pain, love is happiness, love is not just a single emotion… it is the zenith of the whole world. He had manipulated and killed for this day. After crossing the mountain of hurdles, she was finally with him. He just smiled at her and said she looked lovely. His love had matured; it had become quiet, still, deep, calm and constant.

It was summer – the best time of the year in France. The place was crowded, but the Eiffel Tower looked beautiful at night. The twinkling lights made the place mesmerising.

Raghav and Sushmita had booked a night tour in a small cruise. The ride had filled their hearts. The cool wind and the beautiful lights had mesmerised them. They were standing in one corner of the boat, enjoying their drinks and making small talk. Just then, Raghav pulled her closer to himself. Their eyes met and there was a current flowing between them. Raghav slowly whispered in her ear, "May I, please?"

Sushmita did not stop him. She closed her eyes, assuming he would kiss her. Instead, he pulled her closer and caressed her back with his long fingers. He slowly unfastened the hook of her necklace and removed it gently. Very smoothly, he slipped it in his pockets. Sushmita was surprised. She had expected something else.

Raghav had already arranged for tickets to the top of the Eiffel Tower. The view was magnificent. The entire city looked like someone had lit a thousand candles to bless them for a new beginning. Raghav and found a small space that would give them some privacy. "Sushmita, I want to tell you something. I know this has been very difficult for you. It has not been easy for me either. We both have pasts and they are not something that would ever make us happy."

He held her hand and pressed it gently. "I have done some terrible things, and you don't remember what your life was like. You are still confused about a lot of things. I, too, have my set of issues. But we can make a better future together. If only you stand by me, we can have a beautiful life ahead. I understand what you must be thinking. No one would have the courage to think about the future when the past holds so many questions. But you need to have faith in a better future, because no matter what the truth about your past is, it will still remain your past. You cannot change it. I have been madly in love with you ever since I saw you. But unfortunately, we parted ways. It seems that god has sent you to me once again. He has given me a second chance. I feel the almighty wants us to be together, but will you trust me?" Saying this, he went down on his knees, pulling out a ring. "Sushmita, will you marry me?"

The next day, they met at breakfast. Sushmita was wearing the ring that Raghav had given to her the previous night. She had been thinking about her circumstances all night. She was not madly in love with him, but she did really like him. There was no reason for her to decline the proposal. Given her current situation, she did need someone to pull her out, and there was no one better than him. If she had a family, someone would have come to take her home. It had been over four months that she had been staying with Raghav, but no one ever came to look for her.

At the breakfast table, he noticed that she was wearing the ring. He took her hand and kissed it gently. "Thank you so much for this," he said. He got up, walked up behind her, and slipped the necklace he had bought for her in the US. It looked spectacular on her.

The beginning

They announced their decision to his father once they came back. He was overjoyed for them. He knew Sushmita was all that Raghav needed to set his life straight. Their relationship, though, was not as rosy as it appeared. As long as she did not remember her past, things were smooth. Raghav needed to handle her with extreme care. He would have to love her so much that she would choose him over her past, and that was not easy.

Raghav's dad was not aware about the details of the accident, nor had he asked him about it. He was happy as long as his son was happy. But fear kept haunting him, because he knew that it was more than just a coincidence that Raghav fell in love with a married woman and her husband and child died soon after that.

It had been very long since he had seen Raghav so happy. Hope for a better life for a child is such a strong feeling that you cannot let it go. Selfishness is a part of parenthood. You want your child to have the best, and when they get it, you give yourself enough excuses to change the definitions of wrong to right.

The next few days were joyful for all of them. Raghav was madly in love with Sushmita and now he did not have to stop himself from showing it. She had agreed to marry him. Sushmita was also responding to his love. They were creating beautiful memories for themselves. They would watch movies together, dine out, and go shopping. Raghav had also brought a sports bike. They would often go on long rides and picnics. Love was blooming and so was the sexual tension.

Once, Sushmita gave him a tight hug and tried to kiss him. But Raghav stopped her. Sushmita was shocked at his response. It was unusual for a man to react this way, especially when he was in love. "Not now, Sushmita," was all he had said.

Sushmita burst out. "But why? Don't you love me? Are you not attracted to me? You have not touched me once, in all these months. Are you marrying me out of sympathy?"

Raghav decided to tell her what was on his mind. "We need to talk about this. You are not the first woman in my life. I have had relationships with quite a few women. I have dated a lot of them. Sometimes it was merely for pleasure, and sometimes for business too. But in your case, it's very different. I was not in love with them. It was pure lust, and I was always very clear about it. But I really love and respect you. I am very attracted to you and you can't imagine how difficult it is for me to control my feelings when you are around. But I have promised myself that I will touch you only when you are married to me. By doing so, I want to maintain the virtue of this relationship. I hope you understand. It is just a matter of a few months, until we are married. In the meanwhile, let's understand each other better and enjoy our lives. I want you to be the happiest woman ever. I want to grow old with you. I want you to be with me in every memory, in every moment."

Sushmita said, after a pause, "I am sorry, Raghav. It was just the spur of the moment reaction. It's not easy for me. I have come a long way since my accident. It's dreadful to put together the jigsaw puzzle in my mind. I fear that one day I will find out something that will change my life. I question myself, why I should even trust you. As you once said, it's difficult to plan the future when you are not sure of the past. My insecurities, my apprehensions are boundless. But I have decided to give life another chance. I am determined to lead a normal, happy life, because the future is something that I can still control; the past is something that I cannot change."

She paused again and said, "Raghav, will you please tell me everything that you know about the past few years that I cannot remember? I don't recollect anything. I will believe every word you say. At least my mind will be de-cluttered."

Raghav took a breath. "Sushmita, I used to like you years ago. After that, you left the city. No one knew where you were. Some said that you started working for a multinational company, while some were speculating that you got married. But there was no direct contact with you. Slowly, my emotions for you started fading away. But I always liked you. Even back then, I was always attracted to your intelligence, your personality. I was completely in love with everything about you. But since you were away, I had to accept the fact and move on. I always regretted my inability to speak to you about my feelings.

"Just before the accident, you had contacted some common friends and we met again at the reunion. But with so many people around, we hardly got to talk. We had shared numbers. You had called me last, just to share your number with me.

"Immediately after the reunion, you left the city to return home, and you met with an accident on the way. Because your mobile had my number on the recent dialled list, they called me. I thought that this is my destiny; this is god's will to send you back to me. I took care of you after the accident. I tried hard to trace some relatives or friends. I was not sure if you were married. But no one ever reached out to me. It is likely that you were married, but I don't know why no one reached out to me.

"I became a little selfish. I secretly wished that no one came to take you back, but at the same time, I was also prepared to let you go. I had decided that I would wait till a particular date, and if no one came till then, I would assume that you were not with anyone. I waited till that date and then proposed to you. How I wish I knew more about you, I would not have let you suffer so much. But I am very happy you are doing so well for yourself. You have always been such a strong woman. Trust me, I will never break your heart. You mean the world to me."

The dream is finally true

The marriage date was finalised and the preparations had begun. It was going to be a private affair with only very close family and friends. Raghav had taken special interest in planning Sushmita's attire. He wanted her to look exactly the way he had imagined her on the flight back to India from his US trip. That day, it was his mind's trick to keep him going, but today it was no trick of the mind. It was happening for real. He was finally marrying her. His dream girl would soon be his, walking into his life wearing a red lehenga, looking like a goddess of love. Today was the day that all his dreams were coming true.

The ceremony was traditional and all the rituals were followed. The marriage was also registered immediately. She was legally his wife now. The most stunning woman was now his. He had longed for her, cried and suffered in pain. He had lied, and also killed for her, but in the end, it all seemed worth it.

On the day of the wedding, the wedding hall was beautifully decorated with flowers and chandeliers. The beautiful pink and white flowers made the beautiful stage look even more spectacular. The long chandeliers were radiating romantic lights on the couple. The roses and candles were blessing them with their beautiful aroma. This was their moment. Raghav wanted this day to make such a strong mark in his heart. The pink lighting and Sushmita's face hidden behind the thin red dupatta.

This day would be so strong that it would wipe out each and every negative memory from his mind. It was a new beginning for Raghav, to start a life that he always wanted. The holy fire would burn away all his wrongdoings.

At least that is what he thought would happen. If only he knew that the past follows you and your present does not have the power to stop it.

Unlike most couples, they were not raring for sexual intimacy. They were not looking forward to a steamy night. For them, it was more about companionship, about comfort to understand the depth of each other's feelings. They had not thought of anything special for the first night. Though Raghav had thought about this a hundred times, when the time had actually come, he did not want to rush. They both changed into their pyjamas and sat on the couch watching a comedy film, sipping coffee. When they spoke that night, it was evident that Sushmita was well read and had a clear opinion about a lot of things. She was also open to new things and humble enough to apologise and accept things that she was not good at.

The night passed, changed into dawn and Sushmita was cuddling in Raghav's arms on the couch. They had been talking for so long. Sushmita dozed off on the couch while talking, and Raghav pulled her closer on his lap. Memories of her sleeping secretly in the lounge were still so vivid. He had wished for this since that day.

So much had happened between that day and this. The memories kept flashing in front of him. Haunting and questioning, did he do the right thing?

The next day, Raghav got up early and found himself unable to move. Sushmita was sleeping on his lap and was tightly cuddling him. He smiled, thanking god for this wonderful moment. He slowly moved, made himself a little comfortable, picked her up and put her in bed. He kissed her cheek and headed to the gym. He could hardly focus. He wanted to do so much more to her than just a kiss. But she was sleeping like a baby and he did not want to wake her up.

He did some basic exercises and returned to his room. She was still in bed, fast asleep. He decided to make them breakfast and head to the shower. Raghav was not very fond of extravagant food. He was extremely particular about what he ate. He was not like her. Sushmita was a junk queen. She would constantly munch unhealthy food, and surprisingly, she never put on weight. He had seen her eating pizza. That day he was so amused. The woman was able to eat an entire double cheese burst pizza. She would cook different things and had already made him gain weight. He had to stop eating. Rather, he would keep her away from the kitchen. She would cook, then make him eat. If he refused, she would glare at him. He was terrified of her glare and ended up eating whatever he was served.

He had his green tea and reached the shower. Sushmita was still lying in bed, rolled up in the blanket.

Raghav entered the shower and just as he opened the shower, she gently hugged him from behind. This was the best surprise he had ever got. He had never imagined that she would make the first move. He quickly turned and grabbed her tight, pushing her against the wall. He pinned her against the wall and kissed her, moving his hands all over her body. Her soft cream-like skin had imprisoned him. He could not stop himself this time. Today, he wanted to have all of her. She did not want him to stop, either. Nor was she ready to get off of him. She wanted every inch of him. She wanted to feel his strong body on hers. She was wearing the lacy lingerie that she had found in the cupboard, beautifully packed, and decided to treat him. Raghav was right with his choice. The red wine colour had enhanced her beauty. But he did not want her to hide it. He quickly undressed her and allowed his hands to feel her skin. He picked her up and carried her to the bed.

He paused for a moment, just looking at her. She had a body of a woman, a full grown woman, no muscles, just sheer softness packed in radiant skin. Only when his body rebelled against his eyes, he moved closer to her. Today, there was no stopping. They were both greedy for love.

Happy family again

Raghav started work after a full month of romance. He had cut himself off work for a long time now. First, it was the marriage; then, the honeymoon. There were a lot of things that had to be cleared off the table. He had tried hard to resume his schedule as it was before marriage, but had failed terribly. He did not get up on time, did not exercise, did not control his diet and would reach the office late. He did not bother much, but he knew he had to get back in shape.

Back home, Sushmita lay lazily in bed, wondering how she was going to spend the rest of the day without Raghav. She had already started missing him. For the first time in months, she would be all alone in this new place. She first decided to explore the place to make herself comfortable and settle in. Raghav had told her that there would be house help for her – an attendant for the household chores, and a driver who was available only for her.

When the maid arrived, Sushmita was already dressed in a new saree, showing all the signs of her recent wedding. With her help, Sushmita arranged the things that she had carried from Raghav's father's house. After a few hours of setting up, she called up his father just to check on him. She was feeling lonely, so later decided to meet him too. She called the driver and left for his house. En route she realized that the city was quite different. It seemed that she had never been to this place, or maybe this was one more part that got washed away from her memory. She was curiously looking at the tall buildings and the shopping centres, trying to register the route, in case she had to travel alone.

She spent the entire evening with Raghav's dad, like she used to do earlier. They watched a movie; she watered his plants and made some snacks. This house was her comfort zone. Her new life began from this place. Raghav's dad was no longer his alone. She had built a special bond with him and he had become her dad too. He was the only person who loved her, other than Raghav. Raghav came to pick her up in the evening. The arrangement was a little strange for her. She always wondered why his dad could not live with them. But Raghav had very assertively clarified that it was a decision that was made long back and there was no way it would change. She could visit him as much as she wanted, but they would never stay together.

Raghav ensured that Sushmita was never left alone. She never went into the city alone. The driver would always accompany her and would report her whereabouts to Raghav.

His dad had warned him that life will take a different turn the day Sushmita remembered her past. He took every care to avoid the risk of her meeting anyone from her past life. Though they were married, Raghav knew that she was not fully committed. He needed more time to invest in the relationship. Sushmita was not yet ready to choose between her past and Raghav.

There were times when she would ask him questions about the past or the conversation would somehow initiate the topic. Raghav, however, would always distract her and change the topic. After a point, Sushmita also made peace with the fact that there was no point in discussing the same thing over and over.

Sushmita had adjusted to the new life. She had started enjoying her shopping tours and candle night dinners with Raghav. They occasionally went to nearby resorts, spending the weekends making love. Their passion had not yet faded. They were so much in love with each other, like magnets pulling themselves in each other's arms.

When Sushmita would be alone, she ordered books online and read them throughout the day. She would cook or just plant something new in the garden or watch movies. She tried newer ways to pass her time alone, as she did not have any friends that she could spend time with. There were only two people in the world that she knew.

Slowly, the life that was so exciting, started becoming boring. She started getting lonely and felt a very strong need to socialise, but did not know how to start. She had done everything that would keep her mind occupied, but now that she was feeling well, she did not spend too much time sleeping. Hours became longer and boring.

One day she woke up and felt so miserable at the thought of spending the day alone with nothing much to do that she decided not to call the driver. She would take a taxi and would go around the city on her own. That way, she would get a chance to interact with different people and spend time exploring the city. She got ready and left the house without informing anyone. She took a taxi and went through a different route and reached the shopping mall. She spoke to the taxi driver and tried to figure out more places that she could visit.

She entered the shopping mall feeling elated with the feeling of leaving the house alone. Being able to do something on her own made her feel independent and gave a much-needed boost to her lost confidence. The feeling of freedom was so encouraging. It was a very small thing to do, but after her accident, she had not gone out alone. A constant fear of forgetting something, or being unwell drained out her confidence to an extent that stepping out alone was an achievement for her. It had been such a different experience.

After some visits to the shops, she entered the food court. Walking alone in the food store, buying food of her own choice and eating alone boosted her confidence. She no longer felt awkward alone. It had been a while since she had ordered junk food. She usually went out with Raghav and ended up in fancy restaurants, eating fancy food. Today, she would order things she had been secretly craving.

While biting off her burger, she got a call from Raghav. He was very calm but a little worried. "Where are you, Sushmita? You are not at home, you are not with the driver! What are you up to?"

"Oh, Raghav! I was so bored today; I decided to explore the city on my own. I just took a taxi and went around the city. I finally ended up in the shopping complex, had lunch, and now I am heading back home," she said.

"Sweetheart, please don't do this again. I don't want you to be alone, especially out on the streets. It is too dangerous for us. I have some bad contacts and I don't want them to harm you when you are vulnerable. Please understand," Raghav replied.

"I'm sorry, I did not mean to worry you, but I really get annoyed with the driver tagging along everywhere I go. He does not even look like a driver. He looks like a bodyguard and I hate to be watched like this. I won't do this again, but promise me, you will show me around the city this weekend. Not just the fancy places, but also other parts that are not known to me."

"I promise you, darling, I will take you wherever you want, but for now, please head home."

With this, the fear had already kicked into Raghav's mind. He did not want Sushmita to be held captive inside the house, but wanted to give her limited freedom. A boundary that was safe for him. He had already rebuked the maid and the driver for their negligence.

But the damage was done. Sushmita had tasted freedom. She had opened her heart to a life without him. She was dependent on him for the past one year, she needed him for every little thing. But things had now changed. Today, she had got her wings back. Her old independent self had emerged.

She was too intelligent to be confined inside the walls of the house. If ever she went out alone and recollected her past or met someone who knew her, it would put their relationship in jeopardy. As a matter of fact, her memory loss was a blessing in disguise and he had to maintain it, at least to a point that she was so much in love and committed with Raghav that the past would not bother her. Some more time and some more emotional investment were needed.

That evening, Raghav and Sushmita decided to have a movie night. Raghav had made a large tub full of popcorn and Sushmita had made a large pot of coffee. A projector was arranged on the terrace with a cosy bed and a fluffy blanket. The terrace was already illuminated with garden lights. They had selected an old romantic movie that they had seen at least ten times before.

Raghav was slowly and steadily investing in this relationship. Earlier, he had done it out of love alone, but now he was more mindful. He wanted to make Sushmita fall deeper and deeper for him.

The movie had begun a little late. The cool winds of January were adding warmth to their love. Sushmita was sitting comfortably on one end of the bed with her legs on Raghav's lap. The mood was set right – beautiful lights, a full moon night, and a handsome man who she loved more than anyone. She naughtily started moving her legs all over his, giving him subtle hints. A little twinkle in her eyes was enough to arouse him. Rather, just some closeness would excite him. There were times when he would get excited the moment he would see her. Such was the intensity of his love, of his passion. He pulled her legs closer to himself and grabbed her by the waist. His lips and hands were now enjoying her beautiful body. When they were done, they realised that the movie was already over and they had barely watched it for fifteen minutes.

When they woke up the next day, the sun was already up. But they were too tired to get up.

Raghav pulled her closer and gave her a long kiss. Wishing her a very good morning, he smiled at her, saying that he wanted to discuss something very important with her. He would see her again in his home office in an hour.

On meeting her, he said, "Sushmita, I have a plan for you. It must be very boring for you to stay home all alone, doing nothing. If you want, you can start helping me with my business. I want you to consider my offer. I have recently started a software company and I need someone to manage it. If you agree, you could be the managing director. It's currently a small setup with 8-10 people, but if you do well, we could go up to a few hundreds. I have some plans that I can discuss with you in detail. Please think and let me know your opinion."

Sushmita said, "Raghav, are you serious? You know my medical condition. I don't remember many things from my past life. I don't even know if I still remember what I used to work as, what I was good at. This is certainly a big risk. You could lose a lot of money. To be honest with you, I really don't know what I would remember from today in the near future. My mind plays games with me and when leading a business, you need to have a certain amount of memory, and I really cannot depend on mine."

"I understand that you have come a long way and it is still not easy for you. Your mind is a jigsaw puzzle. But just as you are taking your personal life positively, one day at a time, you can do the same for your professional life. You can learn everything again. There is no harm in trying. At any given point, if you feel it is getting too hectic, you can quit. And honey, please believe me, it's your choice. I don't want to force anything upon you. But I don't want you to underestimate your abilities. You have to learn to move on with your condition. That should not stop you in any way."

Sushmita spent the next two days thinking about her response. She was excited and nervous at the same time. She was evaluating all the possibilities and trying to make a decision. By the end of the second day, she was so exhausted that she decided to speak to Raghav's dad and take his opinion.

She explained the whole thing to him – about her visit to the city, how she felt lonely and how Raghav thought about her managing his small company. His dad just heard her out patiently, he did not give her any opinion of his own and he just allowed her to talk. He asked her a few questions and made her respond to them. She spoke her heart out and finally came to the conclusion that she should try it. She decided to start studying basics of a business and asked Raghav for help. She would take three months to read and understand the dynamics of the business and then take up the role.

The very next day, Sushmita started her training. In the meanwhile, Raghav had completed his resort and had laid off all the resources that knew Sushmita and Sumit. He had also ensured that they found other jobs far from the city. There was not a single soul in the office who would know her. He had not left a single stone unturned, not a single risk of anyone knowing her.

Sushmita had made her training plan with the help of some people in the office. She had made a list of all the topics for which she would require training. She decided to learn some fundamentals that would help her in finance, a little bit of quality and tips about marketing. She had already scheduled trainings from external trainers, as well as people who were working within the company. She spent a lot of her remaining time reading articles and references.

Her spirits were elevated. She was unstoppable. She attended training sessions and read. There was always something that she would read or do to get more and more understanding about business. There were times she would sleep only a few hours and yet would hardly feel tired. Three months later, she officially took over the responsibility of the company as the managing director. Raghav's trust in her had done the magic.

She had started working full time now. She would reach office early and would keep working till late, working hard to deliver the projects she was already working on. After delivering the first batch of successful products, Sushmita had started getting more projects. Her employees were delivering good quality software, and her customer base was increasing. In the initial days, she would often spend time with the team to do the testing herself or check the code. She would monitor her deliveries from end to end, making sure that only good products were delivered.

Nonetheless, there were times when there was negative feedback too and some deliveries had to be redone. On some occasions, she incurred losses and barely got returns on the effort she put in. But things started improving over a period of time. She worked hard to create a good image of her company, improving every single day, working towards better quality each and every time. Slowly, the business started picking up.

Raghav had shifted his office already and was now working out of the same premises as Sushmita. They made sure that they travelled to office together. It gave them some extra time to discuss important matters and keep the flame of their love burning. Raghav's plan had been successful. She was busy, and at the same time, she was always around him.

Sometimes they went for lunch dates, and on bad days they would just grab a cup of hot tea late at night at a nearby local tea shop. Raghav always ensured that Sushmita was safe and happy. He never allowed her to stay back in the office till late, alone. If she needed to stay late, he sat in the office too. He never failed to tell her how much he loved her. His love and respect for her had grown over time; she had done a great job with the company. The way she had laid the foundation of her company was remarkable and absolutely exemplary. Despite her illness, she had managed to perform so well. She often got confused and felt lost, but he stood by her and encouraged her to try harder.

In spite of the fact that they hardly got free time, they kept their romance alive. Sometimes they took a few days off and travelled, or just stayed in a nearby resort. They would listen to old music or read books together. Their relationship had become a perfect blend of love, respect, passion and ambition.

❖

It had been over a year that the business was started and it was doing well. Despite all the success, Sushmita secretly longed for a child. She tried to talk to Raghav about it once, but he did not respond. Though he knew that this day would come, he also knew that if she ever visited a doctor, she would find out that she already had conceived and delivered a child. Sushmita was also at a high risk. She was not very young; age would not help the pregnancy and her illness would add more risk to it. He asked her to give him some time to think, just to avoid the topic.

After being patient for a long time, Sushmita finally asked Raghav a question that had been bothering her for a long time. She asked, "Raghav, why are there stretch marks on my lower abdomen? Is it due to child birth? I don't see any scars, but there are stretch marks. Do you have any idea about me ever having delivered a baby?"

Raghav was shocked to hear this. He was just not prepared for this question. He knew she wanted a child, but he had forgotten about the stretch marks. After a long pause, he finally said, "From what I remember, you were quite fat back in college. When I met you after years, you had shed a few kilos, and after the accident, you have really transformed. All this weight loss does take toll on the skin. I have been exercising for years now, and seen this happen to many people. I don't deny the possibility of a child, but that seems really weak. No one ever came looking for you. I already told you hundreds of times, that if someone did, I would have been very happy. So let's just safely assume that the stretch marks are due to the drastic weight loss and nothing else."

"But Raghav, I would love to have a child, a child of our own. I want a child who would bind us together, stronger than ever before."

"Darling, let's just give ourselves some time. We have both been through so much. Plus, I am a little concerned about your health. I don't want you to go through any more pain. So please, wait for some time. We will be ready soon."

By saying so, Raghav smartly postponed the topic again. He had come so far with her. It was just a matter of a few more days, and then he would have nothing to worry about.

A child was not a bad idea. That would bind her to him even more. A woman will have lesser qualms to leave a husband, but would think a million times before leaving the father of her child. He decided to think about this a little more.

Bonded

It was Sushmita's birthday again. Raghav was excited to celebrate it. Two years back, he had to hide and be manipulative to be with her. This year, though, he would openly display his love for her. The last time, he had so many people around, but this year, he would have her exclusively for himself. He had decided that he would like to have a child with Sushmita. He planned to reveal his decision to her tonight.

That would be the biggest birthday gift, more precious than the diamonds he had bought. He had asked a party planner to decorate their house. A beautiful olive green dress lay on Sushmita's bed, paired with a beautiful set of emeralds and diamonds. Raghav was the kind of man straight from Hollywood movies. He knew how to please his lady love and how to keep her falling in love with him.

It was just the two of them in the house. With light jazz music, they quietly had their cognac, followed by a delicious dinner. The cake Sushmita had cut earlier was a small chocolate cake, just enough for the two. While having dessert, Raghav pulled Sushmita closer to him and planted a deep kiss on her lips. He brought his face closer to her ears creating sensuous whirls in her heart. "Sushmita would you like to be the mother of my child?" Sushmita could not believe her ears. She had almost lost hope of Raghav agreeing to this. Especially considering their age, she was convinced that he would not want additional responsibilities.

This revelation brought so much happiness to her. For a moment, she thought she must have done some really good deeds to find a husband like Raghav. He was not only successful himself, but had helped her rebuild a life of her own. She had a successful career and a very happy family. Little did she know that behind all the glory was a gruesome act. She had already paid a heavy price for all that she had now got.

In the next few days, Sushmita and Raghav visited a good gynaecologist, just to be sure that they were physically fit to have a child. Of course, the gynaecologist was chosen by Raghav himself and she was well paid to reveal only those details that were necessary. On one occasion, Sushmita asked the doctor if there were any symptoms that she had delivered a child earlier. The doctor had refused to give a direct answer and assured her that it really did not matter.

Three months after all the treatments and doctor's visits, Sushmita discovered she was pregnant. The doctors had declared that it was a critical pregnancy, and Sushmita was advised bed rest. Raghav was extremely happy with the news, but was equally worried. At no cost did he want Sushmita to suffer. The bed rest was also a blessing in disguise, he thought. The lesser she went out, the lesser risk he had of her bumping into someone from her past. He seemed to have become god's favourite child all of a sudden. Everything that he had longed for in all these years was finally coming true. The almighty had showered all his love and blessings on him. He was getting everything he always dreamt of.

Days passed, and the family was preparing for the arrival of the new member. Raghav's father had started staying with them again to make sure that there was additional support. Sushmita's office had now shifted to her home, and most of the time, she worked from home. Raghav would take up additional responsibilities, if needed, to ensure Sushmita got adequate rest. The whole family was taking utmost care and ensuring that Sushmita was safe, knowing well that it was high-risk pregnancy.

Revelation

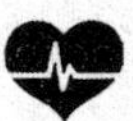

Sushmita had to visit the doctor for her final sonography. Her delivery was just a few weeks away. She entered the hospital and was waiting for her turn. Raghav's father had volunteered to accompany her since Raghav had scheduled some urgent meetings. Sushmita sat in the waiting room of the plush hospital, browsing through some magazines. Raghav's dad decided to just take a stroll around the hospital, followed by a short coffee run.

A tall, good-looking man walked into the waiting room and took a quick glance at the woman reading a magazine. The figure seemed familiar, but he could not see the face. He waited a little longer to see who it was. He got the shock of his life when he saw Sushmita. How on earth was she here? It took him a tad longer to gather strength to go and speak to her.

He had heard that Sumit and Sushmita had met with an accident. Even their little one Amey was with them. The accident was so bad that all three of them could not survive it. It was tragic. They were college friends and had always stayed in touch. Sushmita had married Sumit and thus their friendship had continued. The previous Diwali, he had visited them for lunch, but they had not spoken too much because a guest had an accident. He had to go back to the US the very next day, and had missed any chance to have a further conversation with them.

His college friends had told him about the accident, but no one had ever got all the details. Since Sushmita and Sumit did not have a close family, there was no one to get more information from. By the time the news was out, it had been almost two weeks. Their friends could only mourn their deaths. There was no further news, and soon, the intensity of the matter had faded away. Their friends got busy with their lives and no one really tried to find out more.

Akash could not believe his eyes. If Sushmita had survived, why did she never contact him? What was she doing all this while? Apparently, she was pregnant too. If Sumit was no more, whose child was this? Or was the news fake? A million questions started haunting him. With great will power, he gathered courage to speak to her.

"Hey, Sushmita! How are you? It is so good to see you hale and hearty." He took a pause to give her time to react. He did not bombard her with any further questions.

Sushmita had a big question mark on her face. Who was this man? How did he know her? Was he someone she had recently met and forgotten about, or did they know each other from before the accident? She could not trust her memory any longer. She took a long pause to try to recollect who he was. This had happened to her so many times before. She had decided to give her memory some time, and then react.

She finally spoke. "Hi, sorry, but I do not recognise you. Please don't misunderstand me. Can you please reintroduce yourself?"

Akash was surprised. "Hey, I am Akash, your college friend. How can you not remember me of all people? Where is Sumit? I am so happy to see that you survived the accident."

Sushmita was confused. "Sumit? Who Sumit? I don't know any Sumit."

With this statement, a big frown had appeared on Akash's face. "Sushmita, are you alright? Sumit is your husband."

"Sorry sir, you must be mistaken. I am married to Raghav Mehta and I don't know any Sumit, neither do I know you. So please excuse me."

She said this and walked away to the doctor's cabin. Akash was still waiting for her when she finished the appointment. By now, he had figured out that something was terribly wrong. He proceeded to talk to her. "Sushmita, please give me ten minutes."

He pulled her to a corner. He pulled out his phone and showed her pictures they had taken on the day of Diwali in her house. Sushmita was now devastated. Seeing herself with another man with a child hugging them was something she could not digest.

Akash, however, was now back in his senses. He grabbed her phone and typed his phone number into her phone and asked her to call him. Raghav's father had already arrived, and she decided to conceal her shock and quietly went home. She spoke about how the doctor was happy with the child's growth, and chose not to speak about the matter.

She had prepared herself deep in her heart for the possibility of this. But she never expected this to be true. It had been so long. In her mind, the possibility had become weak and she had accepted the fact that it would never happen. She had also mentally prepared herself that she was never married, never had a child and she had moved on with her life. She was just not prepared for this. The timing couldn't have been worse. The baby was on its way. Knowing the truth was not helping her in any way. But the questions kept gushing in her mind. Who was this man Sumit? Where was he and why did he never try to contact her. From what she knew, Raghav had published her picture in the newspaper along with all the contact information. Did he never read it?

Why would the truth appear now when the delivery was just a week away? The baby was their love. She had dreamt about a happy family with the baby, Raghav and herself. Her father-in law's happiness knew no bound. The old man did not deserve this revelation. Neither did Raghav. They had loved her, accepted her and given her tremendous support during her difficult times.

Sushmita was shattered and confused. There was no denying that she had indeed been married and had a child. But why did the man not come to claim her? Did he not recognise her? But he was her past. Raghav was her present and a happy family with the baby was her future. Should she compromise her present and future for a man who never showed up?

Sushmita was lost in her thoughts day and night. She thought of all the possible scenarios with the man in the picture. No reason was strong enough to motivate her to find more information about him, though. One step towards getting more information meant that she would put her marriage with Raghav at risk.

The baby deserved to be loved and cared for by its parents. Raghav deserved to be with the baby. He deserved to be loved. All that while, Raghav had never denied the possibility of her being married. He had done everything possible to ensure that he was doing the right thing.

Sushmita had slowly and steadily come to the decision that she would never reveal the fact that she knew that she was once married and had a child. She would go ahead with her life with Raghav and the baby. If things came her way, she would deal with them at that point.

Bliss

She had to focus on the arrival of the baby. Raghav had kept the room vacant for Amey at one point, but destiny had played a nasty game. Maybe god had compensated for it by giving them much more. He would soon have a child of his own.

The room was painted with vibrant colours. Toys and clothes and all the baby stuff were neatly kept ready. The family had started the countdown. The topic of Sushmita's past was pushed back. The baby was a very strong reason to take her mind off all the negativity. They had decided to name their son Jay. It was a short and sweet name that meant victory. Victory of love.

Sushmita had decided that she would not trust an unknown man and compromise her future. She would not risk her family's happiness for a truth that no one could prove.

The countdown was finally over. Sushmita was admitted in the hospital. She was in labour for more than eight hours. Raghav stood beside her, holding her hand, trying to pacify her the whole time. He felt terribly guilty for the pain that she had to endure, but that was nature. If only he could take away her pain. After eight painful hours, Sushmita gave birth to a beautiful healthy baby boy. The news was shared and everyone around was rejoicing.

After a few minutes, the baby was handed over to Sushmita. The sight of the baby made her extremely nervous. Memories kept flashing; she felt she had done this before. He had been born before. That feeling of warmth, that enthrallment was not new to her; she had experienced this before. She could now see blurred images of a tiny baby exactly like the one she was holding, and a vague figure of a man. That man was certainly not Raghav. The feeling was intense, and Sushmita felt strange. The helplessness grew as the longing increased. She was feeling breathless. The doctors immediately took the baby from her and handed it over to Raghav.

Sushmita was moved to the ICU immediately. She was sedated so she could rest for a few hours. The delivery was too taxing for her age. Raghav was now in charge of the little one. He felt so enthralled to hold his own child in his arms. Its tiny hands and legs brought in a flood of emotions in him. He had never thought that he would ever feel the joy of holding his own flesh and blood in his hands.

His dad too was elated to see his grandchild. He had been longing for this all his life. Today, his happiness knew no bounds. His only son was blessed with a child. He had suffered a lot. The difficulties through which his son had been had hardened him and made him emotionally unstable. The child would bring back the glory and heal his wounds.

The doctor told Raghav that she was exhausted, and needed some extra care. For the moment, he wanted to enjoy the feeling of fatherhood – the feeling that he would now be responsible for bringing up a new life. He would cherish this moment for the rest of his life.

Within a few hours, Sushmita was back to normal and the baby was handed over to her. She hugged the little one with great love. She was overwhelmed to see the resemblance the baby had with Raghav. The same face, same eyes. But flashes of another child kept coming back to her. The sleep had helped a lot, but had not stopped these images. She kept having a feeling that she had done this before.

Sushmita was now at home. Nursing the baby had become tiresome. She would sleep at odd hours, and was always on her toes. She happened to know many things naturally. Sometimes, she amazed herself, but always pushed away her instinct, thinking no one teaches a woman how to become a mother. Raghav supported her in every possible way. He was an amazing father. For hours together, he would keep holding the baby in his arms. He, too, would remain awake at night when the child woke up. Sushmita and Raghav were enjoying their parenthood. But images of the baby kept flashing. At times they made Sushmita extremely nervous. She would lie in bed for hours, doing nothing. The emotional and physical stress was taking a toll on her health. She had not told Raghav anything about the images of the child; nor did Raghav know anything about her meeting with Akash.

Once a mother, always a mother

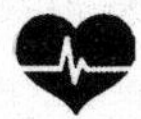

Three months had passed. The intensity of the emotional turmoil had increased. Raghav had noticed it, but kept denying the possibility that it could have something to do with her past. He thought the pregnancy was difficult, which was making her exhausted. He was in denial but Sushmita started getting miserable. The flashes of the child kept her distressed all the time.

One day, after feeding the baby, she had a major panic attack. Images were flooding her mind. A little child hugging her, asking her to carry him in her arms, going to school, playing football, her holding him tightly. Suddenly, there was a gruesome image of this child, hurt and bleeding. He was in great pain and calling her. "Mom, please help me." He was whining. She could feel his pain, but her hands were tied and she could not reach him. Her heart was sinking. Her hands were trembling, she was screaming for help, but no one could hear her. She was locked somewhere, some place where there was no air, closed – like a dark room.

This made her pass out for a few hours. She lay collapsed on the floor with the baby sleeping in the crib.

The baby started crying after a while. His cries became louder and louder, till they became unbearable for Raghav's father. He usually never interrupted Sushmita, and would help only when he was asked. It had been a while that the baby was crying. Wondering what must have happened, he climbed up the stairs to Sushmita's room.

Sushmita lay on the floor, unconscious. The little baby was tired of crying, and the cries had now turned to sobs. The old man was not strong enough to lift Sushmita. He gently picked up the baby and put him in a dry place. He pulled his phone out.

Raghav was on his way back home immediately. The house helps had already brought the situation under control. Sushmita still lay unconscious, but now they had moved her to the bed. An ambulance was on its way.

Soon, Sushmita lay on the hospital bed with tubes running through her body. The diagnosis was still in progress and the doctors were struggling to find the reason behind the problem. All the tests were normal, without a single symptom that could lead them to a conclusion. Yet, she stayed there, like a vegetable, lost in a deep dark world.

On the third day, Sushmita was back to her senses, but the problem remained undiagnosed. Since she was back to her normal self, she was discharged from the hospital, with a lot of questions unanswered for everyone.

Sushmita had become a totally different person after the incident. She did not speak much, stayed alone in the room with the baby, and was hardly her usual happy self. The images of the child would haunt her day and night. She often got breathless, but the medicines worked and she would fall asleep soon. Sushmita was fed up of her situation. She felt defeated – her illness had destroyed her completely. She would neglect the baby and everything around her. She either had the images blasting through her mind, or she fell asleep.

It was a fresh Sunday morning. The weather was pleasant and it was the first time little Jay had smiled at her. He was six months old and resembled Raghav closely. Raghav had turned out to be an excellent father. He would spend most of his time at home with the baby. Sushmita had realised that in the last few months, she had lost her connection with her little one. She made up her mind to push all negative thoughts aside and spend quality time with the baby. She decided to take a stroll with him.

Seeing her attempt to come back to normal, Raghav was very happy. When she said that she wanted to take the baby to the park, he did not refuse. Of course, the nanny would accompany them with the driver to be on the safe side.

Sushmita found a bench in the park. It was under a huge banyan tree that made it nice and shady. The weather was pleasant and the baby was enjoying in his pram, waving his hands and laughing at the birds. There were a few kids playing in the garden. Sushmita decided to look away from them. She was trying hard not get the images back. Just then, a thought came to her mind. Was there something that she needed to know? Was her mind trying to tell her something? Without further thoughts, she dialled Akash's number.

When Akash finally answered the call, Sushmita said, "Hello sir, this is Sushmita. We met at the hospital briefly, if you recollect."

After a little small talk, Sushmita came to the point. "Akash, you must have guessed why I called you."

"Yes Sushmita, I have been extremely restless since I met you. We really need to meet. I will be travelling to India in two months. It's better if we speak face to face, because I don't want to put you in any kind of danger till I don't have all the details."

"I understand, Akash, but I am suffering too much. I see flashes of a child in pain and agony. It upsets me. I cannot concentrate on anything else. I have a baby now, and I have to take care of him. My husband does not have too many details about my past, so he is not of any help. I don't have any contacts from my previous life. You are the only person who seems to have some information."

"Sushmita, please don't say too much on the phone. We may put ourselves in danger. But concentrate on your family, especially your new born. Trust me, we will figure something out as soon as I am there."

Sushmita took a deep breath and quietly walked home. The short conversation with Akash was good enough to give her some hope.

Raghav was home at night. He seemed distracted. Sushmita did not mention her conversation with Akash to him. He finally asked her, "Have you started working again, Sushmita? Is all well with the office?"

Sushmita did not answer the question directly. She made some vague statements and on the pretext of being tired, carried the little one to the bedroom.

Raghav knew that Sushmita had spoken to someone that evening. However, the call was made through internet, so tracing the number was impossible. The caretaker had immediately messaged him about the call. He had tried to track the call history, but in vain. He decided to observe her and then take further action. There was no reason to panic because of one phone call.

The next day, Sushmita got up really early and went for a jog. She was determined to let go of all the images and wait for two months, until Akash came to India. She would take control of her life. Sushmita was not very active, physically. She hadn't jogged in years. But today, she had a strong urge to jog. She went a long way, trying hard to clear her thoughts.

Days were passing fast. Sushmita marked each day on her calendar. Her countdown had started after she spoke to Akash. She was trying to keep herself busy, but she had a strong desire to know her past. This was all the more important because of the visual flashes of the child, and her mental imbalance as a result. Sushmita had tried hard to take control of her life, as she did not want to go back to her days of darkness. If the condition occurred again, she may or may not be able to make it back. This time, though, she was in a better position. She wanted to find out the root cause of the problem. At this moment, she was not even sure if it was just one problem or many more that had contributed to her condition.

She joined office again. She worked really hard, concentrating on the new business. Every single day was a battle for her. She felt lethargic and would want to sleep a little longer. But she knew that if she gave in, she would sleep all day. The depression would make her immobile. She had to fight back.

No matter how hard she tried, the flashes of the little child kept coming in stronger. She had reached a point at which every time she saw those images, she would go out of breath. She would perspire. Her heart would sink and her stomach hurt.

The images became stronger and more real, as if she was experiencing it in real time. She tried hard to distract herself, but every time the images would flash, she would collapse. She would lie down in her cabin and then would go home and sleep again for hours. The incidences started happening more often and were more severe. Eventually, she stopped going to the office. She would stay home. There was a nanny to take care of the little one and of course, she would also take care of Sushmita. When she felt normal, she would spend time with Jay, either feeding him or playing with him. Other times, she would have no idea what was happening with him as she would just be sleeping. Jay was growing, but Sushmita was unsure if she could handle him all alone.

Not once did Sushmita mention the flashes to anyone. She knew that she had to find the answers on her own. If she told Raghav, she would never be able to find out the truth. She trusted him, but wanted to be the first one to know about her past. She wanted to take an unbiased, uninfluenced decision.

In the meantime, she tried to look on social media networks to find traces of her past life. Maybe she had posted pictures of herself. Maybe she had some friends. But all that was in vain. There were no traces of her past life. She also doubted whether her name really was Sushmita.

She tried hard to remain normal around Raghav. She tried to be cheerful and energetic. The problem arose only when she had flashes. She knew what would come next. She would politely excuse herself and lock herself in the room under the pretext of being tired or not having had enough sleep.

The doctors had told Raghav that Sushmita had had the baby late in life as compared to other women. Late pregnancies were extremely stressful. To add to the issues, she had undergone a major brain surgery, so it was expected that she would be a lot more tired.

With this information in mind, Raghav assumed that Sushmita was really just tired. There was no reason for him to doubt that something was changing. He would often be busy and such incidences would rarely happen in his presence.

While Sushmita rested, Raghav took care of the little one. Those were the best moments of his life. His son gave him a sense of fulfilment. He found solace in the thought that he had a great, loving family – a supportive father, an awesome wife and an adorable son. What more could he ask for from life!

Dishonest

The day finally arrived when Akash reached India. The very next day, he decided to call Sushmita. He dialled her number, but there was no response. He called once again, but still no one answered. This confused him. Was she busy or was she avoiding him? It was also possible that she was around someone, and couldn't answer the call. He decided to not call her again.

No matter what the situation was, she would decide. Either she would call or she would not. If she did not call him back, he would conclude that she had decided to accept her present and move ahead with her future. She had made a choice to leave her past behind. But if she called him, he would help her answer all her questions.

Sushmita was an important part of his youth. His first love, his admiration and then his best friend. She had decided to marry Sumit, their common friend, and he had no choice but to accept the fact. Eventually, Akash got a job in the US and decided to take it up. That would give him a chance to be away from them.

Though he had accepted the fact that she had chosen Sumit over him, it was difficult in the beginning. Later, Akash too fell in love with his colleague and married her. He moved on from her, but still kept in touch with the couple. Akash had spent enough time anxiously waiting for the call, but he did not hear from her.

Sushmita's phone rang when she was in the living room watching television with her father-in-law. She did not want to raise any suspicion, so she ignored the call and decided to call back once she was alone. When Akash called again, she was with Raghav and did not want to answer the call again. She knew that Akash would get anxious if she did not answer, but he had to wait. She had to be in a safe place when talking to him.

Two days later, Sushmita got a chance to speak to Akash when no one was in the house. Sushmita's heartbeat had increased and she was getting nervous. Calling Akash meant finding out the truth about her past that could put her present and future in danger. Was this call worth it? What difference would it make even if she found out the truth? She had to deal with it by being emotionally strong, with or without facts.

She ran the facts like a story in her head, trying to make sense of what must have happened. If Akash was to be believed, she was once married to some person and had a child. The entire family met with an accident and her husband and child had not survived the accident.

Raghav said that they had met at an annual college meet, where they had exchanged numbers. She had dialled his number so he could save hers, like most people do. Since Raghav's number was her last dialled, someone from the hospital called him and informed him about the accident. Raghav had reached the hospital immediately. Because her child and husband were sitting on the front seat, they had major injuries. Since she was sitting behind them, the impact must have been relatively less. Raghav rushed to the hospital, took responsibility for her operation and recuperation. She had survived emotional and physical pain that caused her ailments.

Raghav was her college friend who had always liked her. He supported her. He tried hard to trace her family, but could not. He continued to take care of her as there was no one else who would. During her recuperation, Raghav loved her and cared for her so much, that she too developed feelings for him. Eventually they got married and started a family.

Sushmita ran this entire story a million times in her head. There seemed nothing strange to her. It was her bad luck that her family had met with an accident – simply unfortunate. But destiny had compensated for that by giving her such a lovely husband and now blessed her with such a lovely baby.

Perhaps life had given her another chance to improve her future, and by knowing more about the past, she might put the future in jeopardy.

Though it sounded perfect, she could not deal with the images of the child. Her heart, her mind and her body were all aching. Was there something wrong? What was her mind trying to tell her? What truth did her heart want her mind to know? It made her restless. Three hours later, after she had settled her thoughts, she finally got into her room and called Akash. They did not speak much on the phone, but decided to meet for lunch the next day.

Going out for lunch with Akash was a big challenge. The fear of Raghav finding out kept haunting her constantly. They finally decided to meet at his house, since that would reduce the risk of Raghav finding out about it.

How she hated to hide things from Raghav. It was unlike her. But some things are more important than honesty, she told herself. She promised herself that she would tell him everything once she found out what she had been looking for.

Akash stayed in a modest flat with minimal furniture. Of course, he stayed there only for a few days during his visits to India. The house was very neat and clean and had positive vibes. But Sushmita was a little sceptical. It was the first time she was meeting a man without Raghav knowing.

Akash was careful in greeting her. He was extremely happy to see her again, but controlled his emotions. He did not want to overwhelm her. She was a different person now. The chirpy, confident Sushmita was destroyed, and there were no remains of her. The woman who now stood in front of him was a rich woman who had lost herself. Maybe she was a little girl who would always need a father figure to protect her and guide her. The lady, who had been an inspiration, was now leaning onto someone who moulded her the way he wanted. Her eyes had lost the confidence. The spark of independence was gone.

Sushmita sat on the couch nervously, observing the details of the house like a lost puppy.

"Hi Sushmita, I am so glad you could make it. Please feel comfortable. Should I make you a cup of coffee?"

"Yes please, I am a little tired with the travel."

Akash took a short pause. 'Tired?' he thought. She must have hardly travelled for a few minutes. But yes, she could be tired emotionally, tired of fighting, tired of contemplating the future. He made them hot coffee and sprinkled some chocolate powder over it, because he knew she loved it. He wanted to make her comfortable before they started discussing further.

He said, "I understand that things have changed a lot for you, but things are not easy to comprehend for me, either. Everything seems like a puzzle. We have to bring some sense to the story together. What happened with you is so strange. I have been thinking about it, over and over, but have not come to any conclusion."

"Akash, as I said, what I know is that I met with a terrible accident and had partial memory loss. I am in a state where I don't trust myself. I am never sure whether what I remember is my memory or an illusion. I don't know how I know what I do, and I don't know what I don't."

"Sushmita, you have to promise me that you will hold yourself together, no matter what is revealed after our discussion. It could be anything, but you will remain strong."

Akash was a very mature and organised person. He had done well for himself in the US. He knew exactly what he was getting into. He had got a big whiteboard in his room and decided to jot down every little detail that was discussed.

Since it was evident that Sushmita did not know the beginning, he asked her to start from where she wanted. He just wanted to hear her. He had not expected any kind of sequence or logic.

Sushmita started like a little girl. "I am Mrs Sushmita Mehta, wife of Raghav Mehta, mother of an eight-month-old baby. I also run a software firm owned by my husband."

Raghav Mehta sounded familiar, so Akash wrote the name on the board.

"How did you meet your husband?" he asked.

"He was my college friend."

"Do you remember being his friend?"

"No, I don't, but that is what he told me and it seems obvious so far. After the accident, the hospital authorities called him because his number was in my mobile's last dialled list."

"Who brought you to the hospital?"

"I don't know, and never thought about it." Akash wrote 'Question unanswered' on the board.

Sushmita continued, "We have been married for more than two years now. After my accident, he took care of me. He brought me home and nursed me. I used to stay with his father, who is a very good man. Over a period of time, we fell in love with each other. He knew that I had lost my memory and there was a possibility that I could have been married to someone. He waited for many months for the man to come and claim to be my husband, but since no one came, we safely assumed that we could get married. Even later, no one ever came to claim that they knew me. Not before I met you. As soon as I was normal, I did a lot of research to trace my past, checked most social media sites, but it seemed that my previous self was nonexistent in the digital world.

"I went through highs and lows with my psychological issues, and not once did Raghav leave my side. He stood there like a pillar – always caring and always hopeful.

"To be honest, I have also thought about whether knowing my past is required now. Does it make any sense? What will change if I find out all the details? I have been extremely rational. I had almost given up on the thought of finding things out.

"But lately, I have developed something very strange. I get nightmares. I see visuals. I see a small child crying and calling me mom. He is in pain, he is injured and I cannot help him. I feel helpless; something is cutting through my heart. I want to seek help, but there is no one. I shout, but I am in a closed room, or perhaps a car. I have palpitations, and soon after, I collapse. I have not discussed this with anyone. I know my husband will take me to the doctor and the doctor will give me sleeping pills, but no one will ever try to find the real reason. In fact, no one is capable of helping me. I have to help myself.

"Initially, I thought that this is my insecurity with my baby. I had him late in life. With my health, I feel I may not be able to support him. But now, I have concluded that the child I see is not my Jay. He is someone else. This kills me, Akash."

With this, Sushmita finally broke down. She could not control her sobs. Akash did not utter a single word. He just let her weep. After some time, when she was a little more stable, Akash pulled out his mobile from his pocket and checked something.

"Sushmita, is this the child you see in your nightmares?"

The picture was of a happy child wearing some football t-shirt. She was shocked.

"Yes, this is him. He's a little older, but there is a very strong resemblance." Akash knew what was coming next. He took a long pause.

Sushmita asked, "Who is he, Akash? Do you know him? Am I related to him?"

"Sushmita, he is your son – Amey. You probably lost him in the accident."

Sushmita was now speechless. Her eyes filled with tears and she did not say a single word.

Akash resumed, "Sushmita, you were married to our mutual friend Sumit and Amey was your son. You had a very happy married life. You two were totally in love. Both of you had good careers and a very balanced lifestyle. Apparently you met with an accident and they both did not survive it. While you did survive, you had memory loss due to injuries and emotional trauma.

"The good old fellow, your husband, met you and you got married and the rest is history. The nightmares you get are nothing but your mind recovering memories of your child. Sushmita, you are a mother. The love of a mother is inexplicable. Every time you hold your baby, your mind recollects your son, who died. The nightmares are the deep wounds of a helpless mother. Surprisingly, you have no memories of your husband. The love is so deep and intense that it traumatised your mind. I think we have now found out most of the answers. But I don't remember anyone with the name Raghav in our college. We both have been studying together since tenth standard and our friendship continued till the accident. I do recollect someone called Raghav, but don't know. Do you have any pictures of him?"

Sushmita thought for a minute and checked her phone. She browsed through a million pictures of her and the baby, but none of Raghav. It was strange. She thought deeply, but could not think of any possible reason as to why his pictures were not with her. Possibly because she clicked so many pictures of the baby that it did not occur to her to take her husband's pictures too. Raghav was a very shy person. He didn't like to be photographed.

She thought really hard, but it did not occur to her that every time a picture was clicked, Raghav had made sure that it was with his phone, and not hers.

Sushmita said, "I'm sorry, but I don't have his pictures now. Maybe I have some in my old phone." An assumption, again. The fact was that she did not have a single picture of him.

She continued, "Akash, how do you have this picture of my son in your phone?"

"I had got him a T-shirt from the US. You took pictures of him in that T-shirt and sent them to me. I saved it as a memory. Never felt like deleting any of your pictures, especially after the accident."

"Do you have any more pictures of my family? I want to see who my husband was. What did he look like?"

Akash browsed through some pictures and finally found a few. He handed the phone to Sushmita.

With every passing picture, Sushmita's heart broke into a thousand pieces. What had she done to deserve this? She had one happy family. Why had destiny been so cruel to her? Every picture showed how happy their family was. There were not many, because the pictures were taken only during Akash's visits to India. In some pictures, they were eating at a restaurant. In some, they were all carrying shopping bags. When she saw her own pictures, she felt like she was looking at another woman – a woman who was so healthy and happy. The woman in the picture was glowing, shining with confidence.

The last picture of her husband was a selfie that the three of them had taken. Behind the selfie was a blurred picture of Raghav, obviously not looking straight into the camera. The face was not clear, but from the height and physique, it was obvious to her that it was him.

She zoomed into the picture and asked Akash about the man standing behind them.

"I don't really know him well, but let me recollect." After a short pause, he said, "I think he was Sumit's boss. A very rich man, but I found him weird. I remember him because he broke a few glasses and hurt himself. We thought he was drunk, but he was not. I mean, it's rare that an adult is so clumsy."

Sushmita said, "Akash, this man resembles my husband, Raghav."

"Are you sure? His face is not clear in the picture. Don't make such assumptions, Sushmita."

"He *is* my husband. A man of that height and build is not common in this region. His mother was a foreigner, and he has a different body type than most Indian men. I can recognise him from a distance."

"That means, all this while, your husband knew who you are. But he decided to conceal your identity. Why would he do that? I don't see any reason for him to do it. There is something else to it."

"After the accident, I called the company your husband was working for, to get more information about him. But the numbers had changed. When I looked up the new number and called again, there was no one who knew your husband. I found it strange then, but since I had already lost you all, there was no point in digging further.

"I think we should stop the discussion here. There is no point in speculating any further. You have found details about your past. You have an answer to your nightmares. Please accept the fact that you lost your family, but you have a new family to take care of. A husband so loving and caring and a little angel in your arms. Please stop thinking.

"We both may be completely wrong in identifying the man in the picture. Your husband worked in a multinational company. He may have invited people from other nationalities. We don't know. Please go back home. Take control of your present. The past is history, and you have a bright future ahead of you."

All the explanations were useless now. The truth was out. At least the suspicion was strong.

Sushmita was speechless. She took a cab home. The baby was sleeping and the nanny was busy in the kitchen.

Sushmita ran to Raghav's room and started checking his drawers. She was looking for an unusual blue colour shirt that she had seen in the picture. She had not mentioned it to Akash, but she had seen a logo on the collar of the shirt. A logo used by a foreign brand.

This brand sold only in the US, and it was Raghav's favourite shirt. It could not be a coincidence that someone came to her late husband's party wearing the same logo, with the same build as Raghav's. The peculiar blue shirt was neatly kept in the drawer. It was ironed, but not washed. She carefully unfolded the shirt to find blood stains on it.

There was no reason to look any further. She was shattered. Devastated and broken. Her husband, the love of her life, had lied to her. He knew how much she had suffered because of the memory loss. If he knew about her past, then why did he lie? If only he had told her once that there was a bitter truth, she would have swallowed it. She would have made peace with the past. What option did she have?

She had lost it all. Her rationale, her logic, nothing seemed to work. She was furious. When Raghav came home that night, she took him straight to the room and showed him the shirt.

"Is there something you want to tell me, Raghav? You still have time. Please tell me the truth."

Raghav tried his old ways to change the topic. He said he got hurt but forgot to wash the shirt. He gave her a thousand reasons and pretended in a thousand ways. But the look in her eyes was different today. She was shattered. She had lost trust.

She was furious and kept shouting. He tried to calm her down, but she became uncontrollable. She shoved him hard against the wall in anger.

With the loss of control, Raghav lost his temper, too. "I did everything for you, goddamn it! I wanted you, and you are mine, only mine. I will kill the whole world to have you."

There was a long pause between them. He had said too much. He did not reveal in as many words what he had done, but the words were enough to thrash her from within.

Sushmita collapsed on the floor. She was breathing, but not moving. Her body had become stiff. Raghav rushed her to the hospital.

Today

It's now been over a year. Sushmita is a lifeless being. She has lost sense of everything. She has no control over her body.

History has repeated itself. Raghav, a motherless child, is now the father of a motherless child. He did win the game, but at what cost? He destroyed a happy family.

He was agonised at not having a mother to love him as a child, and he gave the same pain to his own child.

The grief is so deep, he may never heal.